SUPERDOLLAR

A NORTH KOREAN CONSPIRACY

BY

JOE BRENNAN

*

Published by OJM Publishers

Copyright 2011 Joe Brennan

This book is a work of fiction. The names, characters, places and incidents are products of the writer's imagination or have been used fictitiously and are not to be construed as real. Any resemblance to persons, living or dead is purely coincidental! Please respect the author's hard work.

****

To my wife Rosemary,

a most amazing woman!

Chapter 1

The door swung closed behind Danny Devine. Daylight retreated from the West Belfast Worker's Club. Danny's eyes adjusted to the murk. The smell of stale beer and sweat mingled. Hushed chatter stuttered for a second while the scant regulars placed and then approved him.

Danny was hyped but calm, adrenaline flowing but under control. The Webley .45 Mark VI tucked into the waistband of his jeans dug into the flesh above his left hip. The big revolver was almost an antique. With it's six-inch barrel, bulky cylinder and hardened rubber butt, it looked like something John Wayne would have spun around on his forefinger. Most operators carried more modern guns; Glocks and Rugers. But Danny was different, he felt firing your weapon was a last resort and the big handgun doubled as a bludgeon. It had cracked many a defiant security guard's helmet. Danny's deep blue eyes swept the room until he found who he was looking for, Gary Doherty, Finance Officer for the Belfast Official IRA, in his usual spot; one elbow propped on the bar of the club lounge. His silver hair almost glimmered in the scarce low-wattage light. His moustache and leather jacket both belonged to the seventies, but he made the look work with that smooth confidence that comes with a bit of mileage on the clock. 1996 and even though The Officials were supposed to be on ceasefire for almost twenty five years, they were still a fully functional private army, and that takes money, big money!

"Right, Gary? Everything set?" Danny touched Gary shoulder as he spoke, it startled him.

"Jeez, Danny, you frightened the shite out of me... Aye."

His nervous reaction unsettled Danny.

Gary's chin jutted towards the corner to the right of the bar. Danny glanced over. Two young guys were sat there, hunched over untouched pints on a round table. One nodded and smiled at Danny. The other raised his hand slightly in acknowledgement. Danny nodded back. He'd worked with the smaller of the two before... he was good.

Danny tapped Gary's elbow. "Right here we go; hopefully I'll be done in half an hour. Make sure there's somebody at the gates of the yard. I don't want to stop and get out or have to blow the horn."

"Don't worry, son. I'll be on the gates myself."

Gary frowned and Danny knew what was coming.

"Look, Danny, there's plenty of young, single fellahs in the movement who can do these jobs. You have Bronagh and the kids to think about. *My* Bronagh."

Danny didn't have time for the father-in-law card. Gary should have known better than to crowd his mind before a job.

"Aye, dead on." Danny said. "I plan a move and send two or three kids out who balls it up and end up in jail or maybe even stiffed. Do you think I want to live with that? No way. I plan them and I pull them off." He then remembered who he was talking to and adjusted his tone. "Anyway, I'm near done. A few more big ones and I'll step down. I've had a good innings. It's almost time to quit."

Gary smiled. "Glad to hear it."

"Oh, Bronagh told me to tell you she was asking about you. Call in for a drop of tea when you get a chance, eh? He beckoned the two boys in the corner.

They got up immediately and fell into step behind him. Outside the club, they turned left on the Grosvenor Road and ducked into a side street just off Leeson Street where the Ford Transit van was parked.

Danny looked around in every direction. He'd learned how to spot anything out of place; a wino lying in the street whose shoes were just too clean; or the old classic -- a van full of cardboard boxes, obviously empty because the suspension was sitting too high. *Aye, empty boxes with a wee cop or an undercover soldier lying behind them.* It amazed him that the cops never thought of throwing a load of sand bags into their covert vans to make it look like they were loaded up.

Everything seemed sweet. As the three drew alongside the white Ford Transit van, the smaller guy jumped into the driver's seat, put his hand under the mat on the floor and fished out the key. The engine burst into life on the first turn, it had been tuned up to the last. Danny settled into the passenger seat and the larger of the two boys sat on the wheel arch in the back. He placed a steadying hand on a wheelie bin full of water that was tied to the inside wall of the van.

They drove across the Grosvenor Road and through the Hospital grounds towards the business park on the Boucher Road. The driver started to sing in a low voice. *Moonshadow*; the same song he was singing on the last job he and Danny were on.

"Cat Stevens fan then, are you?" Danny asked.

The driver looked at Danny, his expression mildly embarrassed. "Ah, no. It's just my lucky song. Always sing it when I'm doing driver."

Danny wasn't superstitious, especially about operations but he said nothing. *Whatever works for you, kid.*

They pulled into the car park of the big department store and the security truck had already arrived. There was some construction work going on at the growing commercial site and the white Ford Transit blended in with the other builders' vans in the car park.

They stopped about thirty feet away from the navy-blue cash-in-transit truck. Danny had been watching it for weeks. First week it arrived Monday morning, eleven thirty. Second week was a bank holiday and it didn't show. But it arrived Tuesday morning, eleven thirty, and Danny could see that the box was bigger and heavier than the box they'd loaded up the previous week. Week six was another bank holiday and sure enough, no pickup on Monday, but the big box on Tuesday.

They planned the job for the Tuesday after the next bank holiday. And Danny maintained the good summer vibe that he'd settled into on his morning jog. Thousands of windshields bounced sunlight in the car park. To Danny, it was one of those bright and beautiful mornings that seemed to make the whole city smile. He people-watched while the minutes ticked by. The first frown he spotted was on the face of the security guard, he cautiously came out of the side door of the store, cash box in hand. He was average height but stocky.

Danny gave the tall boy the nod. Pulling down their masks they stormed the target. The security van was only yards away from the side door. The guard might have had time to run back inside or get the box into the back hatch of his truck but the sight of the two balaclava-clad men stalled him just long enough.

Waving his Webley, Danny yelled, "IRA!" In his peripheral he saw a young family standing by their hatchback. Danny's left hand rose level with his shoulder, palm facing the family. Two twitches of his four fingers dropped them. *That's it. Keep your cool and stay out of the way.*

The tall boy shouldered the guard flat against the wall. Danny snatched at the box. The guard held tight for half a second then the look in Danny's eyes and the sight of the big handgun melted him. He let go of the box and fell to the ground, and covered his head with his arms. Danny turned towards the Ford with the heavier-than-it-looked box in hand. He didn't mind turning his back on the guard, he knew his partner had his back covered.

Danny's job was to get the box back to the van and into the wheelie bin full of water before it started spewing pints of blue dye and screaming like a demon. His heart chugged in his chest. The muscles in his load-bearing arm tightened. Tunnel vision kicked in. Job almost done.

Danny jumped into the van through the open side door. He dumped the box into the wheelie bin. Water sloshed over the rim as it sank to the bottom. He crouched down and looked out onto the car park. The tall boy strolled towards the van with his Glock by his side. He turned around a few times and growled at the guard to keep his head down. Kept a calm head on his shoulders. Then he climbed into the passenger seat and nudged the driver.

"Okey dokey, driver. All's good. Let's go."

Danny didn't mind that his underling had taken it upon himself to give orders. It showed initiative. The driver manoeuvred through the car park calmly and sang his lucky song. Danny liked this wee team.

As they left the car park, the security mechanisms in the box attempted to do their stuff. The jets of dye that should have exploded all over anyone in its vicinity pumped into the water. Blue bubbles spluttered to the surface. The inside of the box had already been saturated so the dye that was supposed to mark the bills inside was diluted and rendered useless as was the tracking device that shorted out on contact with the water.

When they got back to the Lower Falls, Danny told the driver to stop at a house on Ross Street.

"Go to number forty-three, lads," Danny said. "There's clean clothes in the bathroom, change and wash. A car will pick you up in fifteen minutes and take you back to work on the building site."

Their foreman, if ever asked, would swear that the boys had been working there all morning.

Danny jumped into the driver's seat and took the Ford Transit a few streets up the road. The gates to the old builder's yard opened as he approached. He drove through. The gates slammed shut behind him. He switched off the engine and jumped out.

Gary stepped onto the yard. "It went all right, then?"

"Aye, no probs." Danny said.

"POLICE. FREEZE." Danny's heart jumped. He spun on his heel and grabbed for his gun. A skinny scruffy man leant against the door jam of what used to be an office. He was in his late thirties and resembled the fabled Pearly Spencer. A big yellow-tooth smile and a furrowed brow crumpled his face.

"All right, Danny Dee?"

"Ach, Bobo. What about you? What are you doing here?"

"I've come to blow your box open, mister."

Bobo raised his right hand. A two ounce pack of plastic explosives, an electric detonator and a small roll of electrical twin flex balanced on his palm.

Danny shook his head then climbed into the back of the van. He lugged the cash box out of the bin. His lower back yelped a painful protest and he let it drop. A tonne weight, the box clanged onto the van floor and dented the ridged steel. Danny pushed it towards the back door and let it fall to the ground. Gary helped him drag the box over to the back wall of the yard and wedged it into one of the corners lying flat on the ground.

Bobo got to work. He knelt down in front of the box and took the plastic wrapping off the explosives. Then he broke off an ounce and a half and moulded it around the protruding heavy duty lock on the box. He put the other half ounce in his pocket. The small electrical detonator consisted of a little aluminium tube the width of a cigarette and half the length. Two yellow electric wires about three foot long came out of the top. Bobo pushed the small cap into the charge attached to the box. He stood up and joined the two ends of the det' wires to the two ends of the twin flex, taped the two wires separately to stop them shorting off each other and started to walk backwards towards the office door. Danny and Gary stood about fifteen feet behind him. Bobo looked over his shoulder.

"C'mon. Are you girls going to do the tamping or what?" Bobo nodded towards a tin bath full of water with three big heavy blankets soaking in it. Danny didn't want to go near the box. He hated the blowy up gear, but reluctantly he and Gary went over and reached into the bath, they pulled the three sodden blankets out one at a time and spread them over the box being careful not to dislodge the det' from the small charge. Then they lifted an old carpet and threw that on top for good measure.

Bobo took a nine volt radio battery out of his pocket. He stood in the doorway of the office with one wire pinned down on a terminal with his right thumb and the other wire in his left hand. Bobo laughed as he stepped back into the office. Gary and Danny saw him disappear. Then they realised what was about to happen next and sprinted towards the office. The dull thud and a warm rush of air blew past the back of Danny's ears. Bobo had got it right as usual.

With an impish smile Bobo stuck his head round the door. "Ok there then, Danny Dee?"

Danny caught the side of the wee joker's head with a sharp open-hand slap.

Gary called Danny over to the box and pulled the carpet and blankets off it. The lid sprung open. They tipped out the sodden cash and it slapped the concrete yard like a fishing haul. Danny looked at the bundles of cash, two of those bundles would make such a difference to his situation, pay all the bills off and a good holiday for him and Bronagh. The thought left Danny as quickly as it came. Bobo lifted a one-grand bundle and held it up in front of Gary.

"Here, this one's soaking. Will I take it home with me to dry it out, you know on the central heating, like?"

"Aye, go ahead," Gary said. "Sure better still, why don't you take it over to Benidorm with you? It'll dry quicker over there."

"That's a great idea."

Bobo pretended to stick the bundle into the inside of his jacket.

"Put it down, Bobo."

Gary pointed to a makeshift table -- an old shop window security-grill laid atop four concrete block legs. It measured about eight foot by four. Danny got to work placing bundles of notes in tidy rows. Bobo threw his bundle onto the grill and Danny straightened it up.

They fired up an old fan heater connected to a generator and pointed it at the wet cash.

"How much" asked Bobo.

"Ninety." Replied Danny.

"Wow... lovely... sweet as a nut." Said Gary.

"Ninety grand! Sure I couldn't give a shite if it was ninety million, this is what counts." Bobo pulled his social security cheque out and waved it about then kissed it. "This is real money, this is mine." He stuck the cheque back in his pocket, laughed loudly and punched Gary playfully on the shoulder.

The fan heater blew and the cash was drying out nicely. Danny stood close to the warmth and changed into fresh clothes. He was at peace; leavened by the feeling of a job well done. But, as usual, Bobo started to get fidgety, and thirsty.

"Right, Gary. I'll head on here." he said.

Danny pulled a fresh T-shirt over his head. "I'll walk round to the club with you, Bobo." Then he turned to Gary. "Okay, Mr Finance Officer. Time to reimburse me for the wages I've lost."

Gary passed fifty quid to Danny who handed thirty straight back.

"I'm on forty quid a day, Doc. I missed a half day so I'm only out twenty quid."

Gary put the notes away and shrugged his shoulders.

Danny tucked his cash into his jeans and turned to speak to Bobo. Before he spoke there was a thunderous thumping on the other side of the solid gate.

"Who is it?" Gary asked.

"It's me."

Gary winked at Danny then turned back to the gate.

"Me who?"

"Fuck's sake. Jamesy. Jamesy Larkin. Let me in."

Gary strolled over and opened the gate. Jamesy Larkin, in his mid-forties, didn't look a day over fifty-seven. The Belfast adjutant stood with his hands on his heavy hips, trying for, but not quite achieving an intimidating stance. Gary led their senior officer in.

Larkin cast a lazy eye over Gary first then he registered Danny and Bobo with a cross between a sneer and a facial shrug. But his dull face brightened at the sight of the bundles of cash drying on the grill. His socialist values weren't quite on a par with his namesake's; the trade union leader of the 1907 Irish labour movement. This Larkin treated Danny to a sneaky smile.

"Finbarr asked me to come round and check that everything went okay," Jamesy said. "I see it has."

Finbarr, although the officer in command of the Belfast Brigade was Jamesy's superior but it was Jamesy who really called the shots.

"Another good result, son. Well done."

Danny was comfortable with Gary, his father-in-law and a real friend, calling him son, but this greedy, sleekit fuck? What right had *he*? Danny, good soldier that he was, kept his professional face on. "Aye, I know, Jamesy."

Jamesy, pound signs in his eyes, rubbed his hands and practically skipped over to the cash. A pudgy digit hovered over the grill as he did his mental arithmetic.

"I counted that as ninety grand when I was stacking it, Jamesy," Danny said. Then, as he followed Bobo out of the yard, he stopped beside Gary and muttered, "Make sure it all gets to GHQ." Less than a minute in Larkin's company and Danny felt like he needed a shower. Bobo walking alongside Danny just couldn't help it, with a big malicious smile he said. "That's another twenty grand's worth of carpets going into Jamesy's big house this week."

Danny walked on and stared straight ahead.

"Fuck up, Bobo."

Bobo didn't push it any further. Wind up merchant that he was, he knew when to leave well alone. Funds for the cause had become a touchy subject within the ranks of the Officials since the '72 ceasefire, and Danny's feelings were more hardcore than most. He could have skimmed a lot of money from every job he'd ever done and ended up with a house like Larkin's mansion. But then he'd have been part of the problem. Another waster contributing to the perception that the Officials, AKA the Stickies or the Sticks were nothing more than a jumped up criminal gang. Gang? Organised crime? Like every soldier was on the make. Ireland's answer to the Mafia. Huh, he wondered how many gangsters had to hold down two jobs to feed their families.

In the club, Bobo darted straight to the bar. "Two pints of Guinness."

Danny shouted over Bobo to the barman, "One pint and one Coke." He slapped Bobo's back. "I'm starting my shift in here at half one."

Bobo looked at Danny, his eyes wide and his forehead corrugated. "This is *incredulous*."

Danny was amazed. Bobo had actually made it to the 'I' section of the pocket dictionary he'd bought in the Oxfam shop. The wee man had taken the notion a few months back, that if he improved his vocabulary, people would take him more seriously, so every so often he threw one of his new words into the middle of a sentence. Of course, to really impress people, Bobo could have cut back on the booze, but it wasn't Danny's place to tell his friend what to do unless it interfered with operations.

Bobo scratched his balding head. "Like, I mean, you're just after throwing in ninety grand and they're still expecting you to work behind the bar for the rest of the day?"

"Bobo, the committee knows nothing about IRA business. *They make a point of not knowing.*"

Bobo held up his hands. "Okay. Just one thing, though. You're paying. I'm skint until I change my dole cheque."

Chapter 2

Danny was behind the bar polishing glasses when Gary Doherty walked in. He was glad to see him. Things had been quiet since Bobo had staggered out. But he shouted the standard greeting across the club. "You're barred. Get out."

"Yeah, right." He replied.

Gary managed the club. Every one knew it was a RA club, but as far as the committee was concerned everything was above board, that's all they knew and that's how they liked it..

Gary perched himself on a barstool and gave Danny a wink. "The money's on its way to Dublin."

"Aye. Let's hope none of it gets lost on the way down."

Gary ran a hand through his silvery hair. "Don't start kid." Danny bit back his response and poured Gary a pint of Harp.

"Listen, Danny. Cathal Goodall's looking to see a few of the Belfast men down in Dublin tomorrow. I want you to come with me, but you'll need to be on your best behaviour."

Danny grinned. "The Chief of Staff wants to talk to us? We *are* privileged."

"That's the kind of thing I'm talking about, Danny. You're not to give this man any attitude. Speak your mind if you have to, but be respectful about it, okay?"

Gary looked at Danny like he would a scolded child. Then he sighed. "Listen, why don't you knock off early and I'll finish your shift?"

Danny's face lifted. "Jeez aye, that would be great, Gary. I could put in a few hours taxiing."

"Here, wait a minute. Wait a wee minute. I'm standing in for you so you can take Bronagh out for a drink or something. Not to knock your pan in all night for that fucking taxi depot. Take a break, big lad."

"Aye, do you know what? I think I will for a change, thanks Gary!"

The little country pub was quiet, as to be expected on a Tuesday night, and that's how Danny liked it. He sat across from his wife and enjoyed the heat of the open fire. Burning wood crackled an accompanying soundtrack. Bronagh's hair matched the unruly tongues of fire that lapped up the logs. She'd gone all out with the hairdryer. Big twisting tendrils of red cascaded down her shoulders. It was nice to see it set free for a change. Usually she tied it back, out of the way of everyday family life.

Danny's gaze dropped to the slope of her belly, not quite concealed by their table. Their third child was on the way. *Three months to go,* he thought. He tried not to think about money.

"I heard there was a big robbery today. Down on the Boucher Road," said Bronagh.

She sipped on her orange juice and gave Danny a little sideways look.

"Was there?" Danny affected a mask of innocence. "I don't know what this place is coming to."

They both smiled, but it broke Danny's heart a little to see the worry lines across Bronagh's forehead when her attempt at a cheeky grin faded. Of course, she knew the score with Danny from day one. She had been conditioned by the fact that her father was an operator, and it wasn't a secret that Danny was Gary's right-hand man. But he didn't suppose that helped anyway with her darker thoughts. She knew as well as he did that luck played a big part in Danny's freedom.

Danny finished his Pint and got up for another. Bronagh was driving so he could allow himself a few. It'd help slow down his racing mind and maybe allow him a decent night's sleep before the meeting in Dublin.

Danny sat behind the wheel of the Ford Mondeo. Bobo had claimed the passenger seat. Gary Doherty was in the back beside Big Luke. The suspension sat low on Luke's side because of his massive bulk. Big Luke was one of Larkin's cronies, and even though he would have no input at the meeting, Larkin just liked to have the huge bastard around. Danny had expected this and made sure Bobo was invited along. To wind things up even more, Danny had picked Bobo up first so he'd be sitting in the front.

Conversation was as limited on the way to Dublin. But as they passed another road construction site Bobo tried as best he could to get some sort of chatter going.

"Its amazing how much they're developing the *infrastructure* down here in the South, isn't it?"

Danny had seen Bobo take a sneaky peek at his pocket dictionary a few minutes before. He snorted and looked in his rear view mirror for a reaction from the boys in the back. Big Luke stared back, dumb as ever. His jaw hung slack and his meaty jowls flapped with each pothole hit. Gary was half asleep and heard nothing. Bobo's big word was wasted!

Sean McStravick checked his watch. The Belfast boys had just arrived. *Early*. No small achievement considering the security checkpoints and road works along their route.

When they got to the meeting house in Dublin, Cathal Goodall was already there along with Sean McStravick, Mick Rogers and Larkin. Goodall was acting Chief of Staff of the IRA and Sean was his deputy, Mick was also a member of the GHQ staff. There were four others on the GHQ but they usually only attended meetings when there was a vote on some issue or other routine business. Danny and Gary sat down in the back sitting room with the others while Bobo and Luke waited in the front room.

Sean kicked off. "Right, lads. This is how it is. The movement has lost a lot of support and we are still short of money. The Socialist cause in Ireland is as good as dead. Most of the people in the South are too comfortable and well off, while the Provisionals have the North sewn up by exploiting sectarianism and through the massive support they have achieved from the hunger strikes.

We are getting nowhere politically. So, for the last few years, I've been working in a more international capacity and we now have good relations with our comrades in other socialist movements and even some of the socialist Governments around the world. Now, as you all know we were getting fake Dollars from our contacts in Poland a few years back, they weren't great quality but we still raised good money with them although one of the members got caught and we had to pull back. Well there has been a new development since then. The Polish have allowed me to go directly to their source, the North Koreans. The Koreans see America as the main enemy of socialism and communism and have now started to up the ante. They believe they can destabilise the American economy with this stuff, they are starting to see it as just as important as their Nukes. But here's the thing, here's the dogs bollix. The dollars they are printing now are near perfect copies, they are so good they can't be detected by ordinary bank staff. The Yanks themselves have to bring in their experts to identify them. And *they* even get it hard to pick them out. The North Koreans have obtained an intaglio press, I don't know the technical terms but this system is the exact same method used by the American government to print money, they are using the same paper the same optical ink, the same security features.

So now what's happening is this, they are offering us the opportunity to run the operation here and in Great Britain. As time goes on we will be given other countries to work in. But for now we have Ireland and England. Well, lads, what are your feelings on this?"

Larkin spoke first. "I think it is a brilliant idea. Anything that makes the movement money should be snapped up."

Gary said nothing but didn't look too enthusiastic.

Danny spoke next. "Well, to me armed robbery was always a traditional method of raising funds for the IRA and that's why I'm happy to do it. But do you not think that we would be perceived as common criminals if we go down this road?"

Gary cleared his throat and Danny took it as a reminder to tread careful.

"That's just my honest opinion, Sean," Danny said. "But if you and Cathal are happy go with it..." He held up his hands.

Cathal spoke for the first time.

"I can see where you're coming from, young Devine. Sean and I have thought this through long and hard, and if it furthers the left wing causes around the globe then I think we should do it. Times are changing and we have to look at a all methods that are there for us to use in the struggle."

Cathal and Sean were two Republican legends and Danny had great respect for them, particularly Sean. He had worked with Sean for years, and if he was happy with the situation then Danny was willing to go along with the plan. Everyone nodded.

"Okay," Sean said. "So the North Koreans are giving us the dollars for ten pence Sterling that's about sixteen cents to the Dollar, it's a gift. If we're all agreed then I intend going over to Moscow next week to make a deal and bring over the first consignment. That's when you boys in the North come in. We will hit all the banks and change bureaus in the North as quickly and as often as possible and then Dublin and the rest of the South. The seventy five grand that Danny and his lads lifted yesterday will get us one point two million dollars." Danny glared at Larkin who just kept his eyes to the floor.

What happened to the other fifteen, you bastard? he thought.

The meeting ended and Gary left with Larkin and Luke to go back to Belfast. Danny walked out of the back room with Sean and met Bobo in the hallway.

"Ah Bobo, how are you doing?" Sean asked.

"Not bad not bad at all, Sean. Are you buying any drink?" Bobo said with a cheeky grin.

"No, Bobo, I'm not. The aul health's not the best. I'll have a drink with you some other time, when I'm feeling better."

Bobo had known Sean since the early seventies and done a lot of stuff, with him, even though Bobo liked a drink Sean knew it never got in the way of his work for the movement. Bobo had been one of the best explosives men they had during the seventies when they were engaging the Brits and he also knew a thing or two about weaponry, he could handle a submachine gun as good as the best of them. The Schmeisser MP40 was his weapon of choice. Goodall wasn't as sure about Bobo as Sean was, and looked a bit concerned on seeing him.

Bobo nodded over at Goodall, "All right there, Charlie?"

"The name's Cathal, Branigan. Now fuck off back to Belfast."

Bobo laughed.

Sean followed Danny out to the car.

"You can fill him in on what's happening," Sean said and nodded in Bobo's direction.

"What about Goodall?" Danny asked.

"Ah leave Cathal to me. I'll talk to him. You and Bobo work well together. I'll be in touch with you before I go to Russia."

Danny explained the deal to Bobo on their way back to Belfast. Bobo's thinking was to just go with the flow. He had learned through out his years in the movement that you kept your opinions to yourself. The movement was supposed to be a democratic organisation but when the leadership took a decision it was usually final.

They stopped in Dundalk for a drink Danny had a coffee and Bobo his usual pint of Guinness. Danny had gone to the toilet and a while after he returned Bobo said. "It's quite an *intricate* plan that Sean has devised here, isn't it?"

"Bobo, I'm going to shove that dictionary up your arse one of these days. Let's go."

Danny got back home at around six and Bronagh had the evening meal ready.

"That smells lovely," he said as he came in.

"Mince beef and onions with gravy, potatoes, peas and carrots," Bronagh said as she put her cheek out for a kiss. "They're probably having sirloin steaks in the Larkin house tonight."

"Please don't bring that up tonight of all nights I've had a belly full of that subject today." Danny said as he sat down at the kitchen table.

Bronagh said no more and sat down to eat. She knew that Danny was pulling in thousands and thousands of pounds for the Stickies every month and never took anything for himself, she respected him for that, but it made her sick to think that he was doing all the work, taking all the risks, and getting nothing for it, and yet a lot of the rest of the leadership never seemed to be short of money while she and Danny were still struggling with their mortgage payments. She had a good job in a city centre office but was on basic maternity pay now that she was almost due. Danny worked behind the bar all week and even done taxi work at weekends to pull in an extra bit of money that was in between the work he carried out for the Official IRA. Bronagh was ambitious and wanted the best for her kids. She wanted more than the dreary life that West Belfast had to offer.

Monday morning. Danny stood behind the bar of the club, cleaning up after Sunday night's session. He heard the front door open. Sean McStravick walked in along with Gary.

"Come on, Devine," Gary said. "Keep scrubbing and polishing there." He ran his finger along the bar and held it up. "Look at that, stinking. Call yourself a barman?"

Danny threw the wet cloth he was using to wipe the shelves and hit Gary straight across the face. He ducked down behind the bar as Gary threw it back at him.

"Right, lads. Knock it off," we have business to discuss here." Sean said. He never could get it round his head that these boys in Belfast could be totally professional and formidable one moment and then completely childish the next. In the old days things were done in a more rigid manner, but then the likes of Gary and Danny got the job done and still had time for a bit of banter and craic.

"Wait 'til you hear this Danny," Gary said, and tilted his head towards Sean.

"Danny you're coming to Moscow with me on Friday," Sean said as he took the cue.

"You can take one of the boys with you, somebody good who you can trust and rely on and tell them to expect to be travelling. They'll be away for a week or so."

Sean was hoping that Danny would not pick Bobo but he knew he probably would. Well as far as Danny was concerned no one other than Bobo would be going.

Gary was happy that Danny was going to start working in a less dangerous situation and was delighted when Sean told him what had been decided. Carrying a load of fake dollars was never going to get Danny shot and leave Bronagh a young widow or the kids without a father. His thinking was that Danny had done enough over the years to warrant him moving into the upper echelons of the movement.

Danny was flabbergasted but didn't show it. He always played it cool, particularly in front of his father in law.

"Right am I going to need a big furry hat then?" he said, looking in the general direction of both of them.

They both laughed.

A moment later Jamesy Larkin walked in. "Sorry I'm late, Sean. We had a few people over last night and it went on a bit late. You know how it is."

A few people over. What the hell is that? Danny thought. That's like something an arty farty play director would come out with. What's wrong with, 'we all got drunk in our house last night?'

"I've just explained to Danny here that I need him to come to Moscow with me," Sean said. "He's going to take one of the other boys with him. I need a bit of security and I need them to carry the stuff back here."

Jamesy almost exploded. He thought it would be down to him to pick the men who would run the new operation. And he would have had more control on what was going on. Danny read the situation right away by the look on Larkin's face and decided to slap it up him even more. He turned to McStravick and said, "Well, Sean, there's only one man I want with me on this job and that's Bobo Brannigan."

Larkin turned purple with rage. He turned to McStravick and said, "Sean, Bobo was a good man in the aul days but he's a bit too fond of the drink now. You know what I mean, like? I've plenty of good men, good plausible operators just made for this job."

"You're right, Jamesy," Sean said. "Bobo was a good man in the aul days and still is. But how do you know about the aul days? You weren't there. You didn't see the way Bobo could play a Schmiesser MP40 like a violin. You wouldn't have seen Bobo crawling through thirty yards of razor wire to get a blast bomb right up against a barracks wall. The same barracks that most of the lads were afraid to even look at never mind crawl up to. There isn't a barracks in west Belfast that hasn't been on the wrong end of one of Bobo's smoky Joes. I think Bobo will be all right."

Sean had moved with the times but in the back of his head he always had his memories, especially the memory of a night when an operation went wrong and he had to carry a dying comrade across fields while he himself was badly wounded and close to death. So from time to time he liked to put the likes of Larkin in their place.

Danny finished work in the club at five, on his way home he called to Bobo's house, a small two bedroom terrace in Clonard Street, he called to let him know what was happening. Bobo was frying beef sausages, onions and tomatoes. He had four rounds of bread buttered on a plate in the middle of his small square table and a cup of tea sitting beside them.

"Ballicks," Bobo said. "Russia. Fuck, I'd love to go to Russia."

Danny looked at Bobo a little closer and could see his eyes dancing a little. And he thought he got a familiar smell as he came into the house.

"Bobo are you on that aul shite again?"

"No I'm not," Bobo said with a look of indignation. "Not at all. I told you that stuff rots your brain and makes you paranoid. No, not at all."

Danny looked over at the TV and clocked a massive joint burning in an ash tray on the unit.

"Dead on, Bobo. What's that?" Danny pointed at the smouldering joint.

"Where the fuck did that come from?" Bobo said in a surprised tone. Then he turned to Danny and said, "Ach well, a wee smoke now and again does no harm, now does it Danny Dee? Does it? Does it, Danny?"

Bobo shuffled towards Danny like a boxer in the ring and threw a few feeble punches in Danny's direction, still holding the spatula he was using to cook with and the hot fat flying off it. Danny couldn't help but laugh even though he knew that it was the reaction Bobo wanted.

"Come on, Dee Dee. Have a sausage sandwich." Bobo said as he turned back towards the cooker.

"No, you're all right, Bobo," Danny said as he looked around at the less than sterile conditions of Bobo's wee house. "No, Bronagh will have something ready for me when I get home. I'll see you in the morning."
"Suit yourself." Bobo said. He lifted the joint and took a deep drag from it. He didn't hear Danny leave as he sat the joint into the ashtray and went back to his now burning sausages.

"Fucking Russia." He said as he spilled the contents of the pan on to a big white plate.

Next morning Danny was back at Bobo's place. After banging on the door for ten minutes and ringing the door bell which had degenerated through time from Westminster Chimes, to a sharp buzz, Bobo eventually appeared. He was a sight, as he stood trying to look at Danny through the morning light.

"Jesus, look at the state of your eyes, Bobo," Danny said.

"You think they're bad from where you're standing? You should see them from my side."

Bobo continued to try and focus on Danny through the bright sunlight and held his hand up for shade.

"Come on on in, Danny."

Danny followed Bobo into the house. The place was bad at times but this time it was a complete tip.

"Look at the state of this place, Bobo. It's piggin'."

"Oh I can explain that. What would Larkin say? 'I had a few people over and it went on a little late.'"

"What time is it anyway?" Bobo asked.

"It's half nine."

"What! Danny, that's the middle of the night. What are you getting me up at this time of the day for? Now you've messed up my whole routine, I'll have to have a siesta or something to get me through the day. You're doing this for a laugh aren't you?"

Danny smirked then threw a hundred quid on to the sofa.

Bobo's eyes lit up. "What's that for?"

"Doc gave me that this morning, Sean said we have to get ourselves some new gear, a suit, a couple of shirts and a pair of shoes each, I'm heading down to Burtons, I haven't time to wait on you, so you get a taxi down and I'll see you later in the club.

Danny got home around twelve. He took his purchases upstairs and tried them on. Burtons had one of their many sales on and he got a nice dark grey suit for fifty five quid, not top quality but smart, he put it on with the shirt and tie set, and the black brogues. As he looked at himself in the mirror on the wardrobe door Bronagh walked in.

"My God, Danny, you look fantastic. Oh my God I think I really fancy you again."

Bronagh hadn't seen Danny in a suit since their wedding day, and she couldn't help thinking, wouldn't it be lovely if Danny was going to work in that suit on legit business instead of some wild escapade. Danny had told her he was going away for a week or so on Friday he didn't go in to detail but she knew something was going on.

Thursday night Bobo came into the club for a drink and to find out what the final arrangements where. Danny had just finished his shift early behind the bar and came round to the other side to sit beside Bobo who had his nose stuck in a big cold pint of Guinness.

"Do you know any Russian?" Bobo asked.

"Not a bit," said Danny. "But Larkin might be able to teach us some before we go. He seems to have a great interest in the place.

Danny had just taken a long draught of his pint when Larkin came in.

"What are you doing on this side of the bar, are you not supposed to be working?"

"Nah, you're wrong there, you see I got off early tonight I've a lot to do tomorrow."

"Aye? I got the night off too, Jamesy. I've a lot to do too. Sure we're international now, you know, shaken not stirred an all that stuff."

"Sean must be mad for taking you two clowns on board. I'll be watching to see how quickly you two mess things up."

"Mess things up? Tell me this, Larkin, what the fuck happened to the other fifteen grand that was supposed to go to Dublin last week?"

Larkin was caught off guard and stammered as he tried to come up with an explanation.

"Aye, yeah, well it was decided we needed to hold back a bit for the units here in Belfast. Expenses and stuff."

Danny glared at him with disdain. Larkin recovered his confidence enough to pull rank on Danny.

"Listen. *You* don't question me about army matters. I'm your superior and I ask you the questions."

Danny turned away from Larkin and said to Bobo, "Come on. We'll go somewhere for a bit of peace to enjoy our drink."

"Yeah," Bobo said. "Why don't we go to the Europa Hotel for cocktails?"

Danny winked at Bobo. "Aye. Shaken, not stirred."

The pair left and drove to Bobo's house and sat outside for a moment.

"Well," Danny said. "Sean filled me in a bit on what's happening here. It seems we're going to The North Korean Embassy in Moscow, on Party business. Sean's meeting some members of the North Korean Workers Party in one part of the Embassy. Where he'll be talking to the diplomats and all that craic. I think we're going to get our dinner there."

"I hope it's stew," Bobo said.

"Then after we meet the Party members, we go to another part of the Embassy to meet with members of the Government agencies to talk the real business. Listen, Bobo, this is big stuff. Sean's talking telephone numbers. We're talking millions here."

"Hold on there, Danny. Hold on a wee minute. I'm not signing off the dole for nobody. That social security money is the one wee thing in life I can rely on. When that cheque comes through the door every second Tuesday, the birds start singing in the trees, the sun shines and everything is sweet." "Look, Bobo, you will need to be a bit more sensible during this trip. Sean and myself are sticking our necks out for you, and Larkin is just busting his chops to be able to say I told you so."

Bobo said, "All right. No problem, Danny Dee. And you don't have to tell me. I've worked it out for myself that I'm going to have to go without blow for the next week or so."

"You got it, mate."

Danny left Bobo and headed home to Bronagh. He lived in a small development of sixteen three bed semis on the outskirts of west Belfast. It was still early and he wanted to grab the last few hours in their local before he left in the morning.

When he got home they organised the girl next door to baby-sit and took a quick trip down to the wee pub. Bronagh enjoyed the few drinks they had and noticed Danny was getting a bit tipsy.

"So you fancy me all over again do you? What I want to know is when you stopped fancying me. The best looking fellah on the Falls Road. Tell you what I'll put that suit back on me when we get back home, eh? I might get lucky."

"Aye? I hope you don't think you're going to get lucky over there in Russia or wherever you're going, you only tell me half the story, and you know something, you've got a big head on ye since somebody told you in your taxi that you looked like Daniel Day Lewis. I'll be watching you."

The banter continued on for a while and in between Danny would get all serious and sentimental, telling Bronagh how much he loved her, and how one day they were going to get a better life for the kids and a better life for themselves, maybe even sell the house and move abroad.

Those little discussions and plans always sounded so lovely to Bronagh, but now it was time to go home. As she drove to the house Bronagh was still thinking how lovely it would be if Danny was putting that suit on in the morning to go to work in a nice office job.

Danny called for Bobo at around ten on Friday morning, this time Bobo was up and ready, he always was when it came to army work. As Bobo opened the door Danny couldn't believe what he was seeing; Bobo standing there in a pure white suit, with matching white shoes, a blue shirt and a pink tie. The suit was two sizes too big for him and sort of didn't move until a few seconds after Bobo did.

"Stop messing, Bobo. We haven't got time, go in and get changed."

"What are you talking about? This is me. This is my new image."

"Bobo, stop carrying on. Please tell me you're messing."

"Listen, kid, if you had the price of this suit you could take a month off work," Bobo said half seriously.

"Look, just get into the car. We're meeting Sean at Dublin Airport in two and a half hours." Danny looked at Bobo and shook his head. "McStravick isn't going to like this."

They met Sean in the departures lounge. "Jaysus Bobo what are you wearing?"

Bobo threw back his shoulders and straightened his tie and cuffs. "Ha I knew you would like it Sean, you're a man of taste and style too."

He turned towards Danny, tilted his head back and looked down his nose at him. Sean just shook his head in resignation and turned to Danny.

"Right Danny, here's your tickets and booking confirmation for the Moscow Sheraton." He handed Danny a brown envelope stuffed with the tickets and a fax from the Sheraton. "I'll be staying at the Metrapol. Right you and Bobo are flying direct to Moscow I'm going to Birmingham first so I'll be a half a day behind you. I'll call to your hotel the day after you arrive."

Sean went downstairs to arrivals and waited until he knew the boys had boarded before going back up to departures to wait for his own boarding call.

Chapter 3

Bobo hadn't travelled much over the years, apart from two package holidays. One to Santa Ponsa and one to Benidorm in Spain. He'd enjoyed what he could remember about the Santa Ponsa trip, although he thought there was just too many Belfast people there. What he could remember of the Benidorm trip, was a touch of class. Far better than Santa Ponsa.

He could remember that the bins he was puking into were much cleaner in Benidorm. The Russian trip was completely different. It was probably a lot to do with the fact that he got on to the plane relatively sober, thanks to the vigilance of Danny, but also it was even more classy than Benidorm.

Danny relented and let Bobo have a few on the plane and after a while he was fast asleep. Danny read the few papers he had picked up in the airport and enjoyed the meal, he didn't bother to waken Bobo. It was just too peaceful.

The plane started it's descent into Sheremetyevo Airport, Moscow. Danny poked an elbow into Bobo's ribs.

"Right, Miami Vice. We're nearly in."

For a moment Bobo didn't know where he was and gazed around. He couldn't understand what the noise was and why his ears felt funny. Then he remembered. He punched Danny on the shoulder.

"International, big lad. International. We are international."

The plane landed and they made their way to passport control. Bobo was a few paces in front of Danny and reached the small booth that contained the Russian immigration officer. Bobo held up his passport to the window of the booth level with the officers face without stopping and attempted to walk on past.

The Russian yelled, "Halt." He banged on the glass and pointed down at the slot at the bottom.

Bobo slightly startled came back. "Sorry about that mucker, sorry. Here you are."

Bobo slid his passport to the Russian who opened it, looked at the photo and then at Bobo who treated him to a big yellow toothed smile. The Russian slammed the passport back down on to the small wooden counter at the bottom of the window and waved Bobo on. Bobo lifted the passport and held it up and smiled again.

"Thanks now mate, thanks, sorry about that." As he got past he mumbled, "Grumpy cunt."

Danny stepped up next and set his open passport on the counter and the Russian just pushed it back at him and waved him on. They made their way into baggage reclaim and waited for their cases to come through. After ten minutes or so there cases came round. They grabbed them off the carousel while Danny looked for the exit.

"Well what now big fella what will we do next?" Bobo asked.

"C'mon there'll be taxis parked outside" Danny said, as he walked towards the big exit doors. They weren't hard to find, the chill wind blowing through was enough to locate them.

Outside they found the taxi rank, three or four east European rust buckets sat there. The driver of the one at the front got out and beckoned them forward and opened the boot for their cases, Danny and Bobo got in.

Danny said slowly. "The Sheraton Palace Hotel, Yamskaya Street, please."

The taxi driver nodded but Danny noticed he didn't switch the meter on. As they made their way to the hotel through the Moscow avenues and streets Bobo's eyes were wide open.

They pulled up at the magnificent Sheraton. The big grey, silver and glass building sat on the corner of two main roads. It loomed. Danny tried to pay the taxi driver. He produced a handful of the roubles Sean had given him for the minor expenses he might incur while waiting for him to meet up with them. Danny knew that Sean had given him the equivalent of about two hundred quid and so he had produced what he thought was about twenty quid, the Taxi driver looked at Danny's notes and made a sign that it was not enough and to come up with more.

Danny looked towards the main entrance of the hotel and spotted a doorman who seemed to be taking an interest in the situation. Danny called the doorman over to the Taxi.

"Do you speak English?"

"Yes, sir," said the doorman.

"We've just come from the airport. How much do I pay him?"

The doorman turned to the taxi driver and spoke to him in Russian. The taxi driver raised his voice in reply. The doorman stood straight and firm as he dealt with the taxi driver. He looked at the notes the Taxi driver already had in his hand, and quickly snatched them off him. He turned to Danny and reached over to the notes Danny held in his hand and took a smaller denomination from him and gave it to the taxi man, who started screaming abuse at the three of them before driving off. The doorman handed Danny his money back.

"Taxis are very cheap in Russia." He turned his attention to Bobo who was struggling with their two cases.

"Let me take those for you, sir." He reached for the cases and took them from Bobo with ease. "My name is Cyrus. Let me know if you need anything." He looked Bobo up and down. "That is a very fine suit you are wearing, sir."

As they all went towards reception Bobo's smile was ear to ear. "Didn't I tell you, Devine? Didn't I tell you?"

The smile and look of satisfaction turned to awe as Bobo walked into the reception and looked around at the splendour of the Moscow Sheraton Palace.

"Shaken not stirred, Dee Dee" Bobo said. "Shaken not stirred."

Danny went to the desk and was greeted by a rather beautiful girl with long blonde hair and a smile as big as Bobo's but with brilliant white teeth and not greenish yellow as was the case with Bobo.

"Good evening, sir," she said to Danny. "Do you have a reservation?"

"Aye. I mean, yes." Danny handed her the fax. *Oh Lord I would be in deep, deep shit with Bronagh if she was watching this scenario.* He stole a sneaky glance down her low cut top. Danny looked round at Bobo and watched him talking to the doorman. God knows what crap he was spouting.

"Where's the best place for a bit of craic around here mate?"

Cyrus frowned. "I'm sorry sir I can get most things for you but I do not get involved in hard drugs, and I must warn you if you are caught in Moscow with drugs like crack or cocaine you will go to prison for a long time."

"No no, not drugs. Craic means singing and dancing you know, a bit of aul craic." Bobo said and did a few steps of a gig.

The girl behind the desk looked past Danny at Bobo and burst out laughing. Danny turned around and caught the sight of Bobo and the confused look on the doorman's face.

"Bobo," Danny hissed throwing him a look that said, "Behave yourself."

Bobo noticed the beauty behind the desk for the first time and stood up straight, threw his shoulders back and said to Cyrus.

"If she plays her cards right she could get lucky tonight."

Cyrus caught the gist of what Bobo had just said and tried not to laugh, instead he nodded in agreement.

When the receptionist finished checking them in she handed Danny the key to their room and they went to the elevator. Cyrus had taken his leave from Bobo and had already made his way to a service elevator and was at their room with the door open and their cases sitting by the massive twin beds. Danny walked into the room and was really set back. It was amazing. Bobo didn't rush in as he wanted another few words with Cyrus. Danny turned around just inside the room and handed what he believed to be about fifteen quid to Cyrus.

"Really, there is no need, sir."

Danny pushed it further towards him and he took it with a grateful smile. Danny just wanted to get into one of the luxurious beds and get a few hours sleep. But Bobo who had slept all through the flight was as bright as a button. He wanted to explore these salubrious new surroundings.

As Danny headed towards the bathroom Bobo turned to Cyrus and said, "Here, mucker. What time do you knock off at?"

Bobo sat at the front foyer bar he had been there for about forty-five minutes on his own. He hadn't had too much to drink as he had been spending most of the time looking at the marble pillars that supported the magnificently carved gilt plinths which in turn supported hand carved stone balconies all around the ground floor of the hotel. He had turned around to take another sip of his new found tipple of genuine Russian Vodka when Cyrus pulled a stool out from the bar beside Bobo.

"Ach, what about ye big lad?" Bobo leaned back in an exaggerated awestruck pose to look up at his new Russian friend. "What are you having there, mate?"

He pulled out some of the notes that Danny had given him earlier. The big Russian had discarded his stiff doorman's uniform and was wearing a pair of genuine Levis and a Nike T-shirt finished off with a pair of Nike Air runners.

"No, please, Bobo, I get good discount when I pay for drinks at the bar. So I will buy for myself."

Cyrus called for vodka and water and handed the barman roubles to the value of around twenty five pence.

"Here what the fuhhh, what did you give him for that drink there? That was about forty pee sterling, I'm paying two quid a touch here!"

"Yes I get good rates at the bar because I am staff, it is normal."

"Aye is that right, well here's normal, you're buying for the rest of the night, aul hand."

Bobo thrust a fistful of Russian notes into Cyrus's hand and sat back defying him to try and hand the money back.

For the rest of the night Cyrus ordered the drinks and paid for them, much to the amusement of his colleague behind the bar who was only too happy to keep setting them up.

Cyrus who was well known to hold his drink well, started to slowly give in to the laws of gravity and Bobo had felt for once in his life he had drunk enough too.

Bobo called to the barman, "Here, mate, I'm going to hit the sack." As he pointed towards the ceiling. "Can you look after the big fellah here?"

The barman nodded. Bobo went to his room and the barman lead Cyrus into the staff room at the back of the bar where he fell into a makeshift bed which was reserved for the night porters.

Nine thirty the next morning Danny heard the phone on the bedside locker ringing. He snatched it from the receiver and mumbled a greeting.

"Well, Danny, how are ya?" Sean asked. "I'll be down in the breakfast room if you and Bobo want to come down, but don't be long now."

Danny hung up and looked over at Bobo, who was sprawled out on top of the bed. His charity shop Miami Vice suit draped over the footboard, along with the blue shirt and pink tie. One scuffed brogue dangled from Bobo's left foot. It's match was out of sight. Danny rose up on the bed, swung his legs round and planted them onto the floor. He put his hands on his knees and pushed himself up straight. Took a long, deep breath. The twinge at the top of his stomach that always came with waking without Bronagh beside him faded.

Danny stood over the sleeping Bobo. He sighed at the thought of waking this international operative stretched across the plush bed on which he'd been farting, scratching and drooling all night. Danny gritted his teeth and yanked the duvet from under Bobo. The unconscious bag of bones hit the floor with a thump but lay still as a corpse.

Danny rounded the bed and put his foot on Bobo's shoulder to nudge him awake. Suddenly Bobo grabbed his ankle and sunk his teeth into Danny's calf. He yelped and tried to pull his leg from Bobo's grip. Bobo held tight. Growled between bites.

"Say you're sorry, Devine." Then he gnashed down on Danny's leg again.

"Ah, Jesus. I'm sorry, Bobo. I'm sorry."

Bobo let go, rolled away from Danny and rose to his feet.

"You can't make an ejit out of Bobo and get away with it. You should know that Danny Dee."

Danny sat on the bed and rolled up his pyjama leg. Little purple moons had risen on the back of his calf.

"Well, do you want to get showered first or what?" Bobo asked. Danny crinkled his brow. He knew Bobo had no intention of going near the water. The wee stinker always said, "I take a bath every six months, whether I need it or not."

The two got down to the breakfast room where they found Sean and another man that they had never met before.

"Well, Danny. Bobo. How are ya?" Sean nodded towards the stranger sat beside him. "This is Anton. A good friend of mine. He knows his way around."

Anton was over six foot, stocky but still very fit. Thick black hair, dark skin and even darker eyes. The black leather jacket he wore was almost uniform to both the ex-KGB and the Russian Mafia. He was born in a little village called Chatva on the Georgian Black Sea coast and grew up there. He joined the local police force for a few years before he was recruited by the KGB and moved to Moscow.

Danny shook hands with Anton.

Sean went on, "Anton's an ex-KGB officer and has been very helpful to us in the past."

Bobo nudged his way past Danny and stood in front of Anton. Sean opened his mouth, as he was about to introduce Bobo, who didn't wait. He shot his hand out and grabbed hold of Anton's.

"The name is Bond. James Bond."

"I see we have a joker with us." Anton said in his wide Georgian accent. "A sense of humour is good as long as it doesn't get in the way of more serious matters."

The four left the hotel and got into Anton's car which was parked outside. Sean got into the front with Anton driving and Danny and Bobo in the back. Before they drove off, Anton touched Sean's arm and quietly said, "under the seat". Sean put his hand under the seat and pulled out a Mac-10 machine pistol. Sean glanced at it and slid it back under the seat. "Insurance" said Anton. The big Lada Riva Jeep was a touch of luxury by Russian standards. As they pulled up at the embassy the guard in the box just inside the entrance opened the electronic gates and waved them through. They were expected. As they drove in to the compound, it was more like a military base than an embassy, and entry was by invitation only. Danny watched Sean's face from the back seat as they went through the grounds. His expression didn't budge. Just another day on the job to him. Bobo was a different matter. He was stuck to the window like a Garfield toy on rubber suckers. Danny pushed his friend's balding head out of the way to get a better look.

Mosfilmaskaya Street in the Rameskin area of Moscow is where most of the embassy and consulate buildings are situated and the North Korean embassy is the biggest, China's being second.

They parked at the side of the main building and walked to the front door. As they reached the steps to the large wooden double doors one of them opened to reveal a small Asian man dressed neatly in semi-formal attire. He bowed slightly to the four. In perfect English, he said, "Welcome. Our first secretary awaits you. Please follow me."

They went up the steps and through the doors into a large reception area. The interior of the Embassy, unlike the grandeur of the outside of the building, was slightly tired and worn but was evidently beautifully put together at one time. They followed the small man down a long corridor, passed ten or so offices on each side and at the end they came to the larger double doors of the office of the first secretary.

Their guide led them into the office and went back out to wait at the other side of the door. The secretary sat on a massive and sumptuous high-back leather chair behind a rosewood hand-carved desk.

Even though he was well above the average height of North Korean males the big chair and desk miniaturised him. He got up and moved around to the front of the desk and bowed in the direction of Sean and the others. The four responded in kind, though Bobo's bow was a little more pronounced than the rest. He then put his hand out to Sean.

"Welcome, Mister McStravick. Our Dear Leader Kim Jong-il sends his most high greetings to you and your comrades in the Socialist Workers Party of Ireland. He also says that his father, the Great Leader Kim Il-sung, always spoke highly of you and for this reason the Democratic Peoples Republic of Korea will always welcome you and your people and help you in your work as best they can."

"Thank you Yon Chang-li" Sean said.

As the handshake ended Sean said, "Mr Secretary. Please tell your Dear Leader that I send my condolences to him on the death of his father, The Great Leader. He was a brave man and a true revolutionary. And let your Dear Leader know I hope to meet him in the near future. I believe we can work together just as I did with his father."

Sean then introduced Danny and Bobo as comrades and representatives of the Party. Anton was not introduced and like Bobo stayed silent during the meeting.

Danny listened carefully to everything that was said during the two hour discussion and made suggestions and asked questions on various points.

When it ended they got up and left the office, their guide was waiting outside the door for them and invited them to follow him. Sean asked him his name.

"You can call me Chi."

They passed through the reception, and made their way down another long corridor to the other side of the building. Half way down this corridor they came to a set of double steel doors. They stopped at the doors and Chi turned around and faced back in the direction they had come and waited. Sean walked up to the door and looked up at a small camera above them and nodded. The doors opened automatically.

Inside this part of the building they were met by three armed military guards. The enclosed area they stood in measured about fifteen square feet. It acted as an airlock to the main reception area which was nothing like that in the other side of the building. One of the guards stood behind a counter to the left holding a sub machine gun. The other two guards motioned for the visitors to step forward to be frisked.

After the search another steel door to the right was opened and they stepped through into another section of the reception area. They were met by Yang Li who walked over to Sean and smiled as he embraced him.

"How are ye, Yang?" Sean asked. The Irish greeting mixed with the Oriental name sounded strange to say the least.

Sean stepped back and they walk side by side down another corridor. The walls were plain and painted uniform grey. The floors were well worn from the constant traffic of busy operatives walking from one office to another. The doors looked like they were about to fall off their hinges. Inside these offices there was a constant chatter from people on the phone. Others sat behind computers both punching in and retrieving data while a steady flow from desks to filing cabinets never seemed to stop.

They got to the bottom of this corridor and Yang Li's office was situated in the same position, and was the same dimensions of the secretary's. But it was nowhere near as relaxed and plush. It was a work place.

Unlike the secretary, Yang Li had immediately acknowledged Anton and greeted him in Russian. Sean introduced Danny and Bobo and Yang shook hands with them. He turned to Sean.

"Sean. You're comrades in the IRA are great fighters and they are legendary among our people we have learned from your tactics and follow your methods closely. But please Sean, do not expect us to follow your style of dress." He nodded towards Bobo. Everyone burst out laughing except Bobo.

Sean took Yang to a far corner of the office and spoke with him for a few minutes in whispers. Then he turned to Anton and called him over. Anton pulled a plastic bag stuffed with Sterling out from under his shirt. Sean did the same. The money seemed to come from nowhere and Danny reprimanded himself for not registering the fact that Sean had looked so much heavier that morning.

Sean produced a total of one hundred thousand sterling and laid it on the table, Danny knew that seventy five of it was from his handy work the rest probably was scraped up through army funds.

Yang looked at the cash.

"This is peanuts, Sean. We have to aim higher to make this attack on the western capitalists effective. Sean, I should be giving you one point five million dollars for this money but today I have made instructions for you to receive two million as a token of our commitment to you and to assist you on your move towards the cause of worldwide socialism."

Yang scooped the sterling into a large cardboard box, lifted an internal phone from his desk and spoke briefly. After a few minutes two men came in carrying a grey box each. The boxes were about two foot by twenty inches by ten inches they were made of sturdy cardboard and the lid was fastened to the box by elasticised belts with black steel hooks clipped to the sides. They sat the boxes on one of the desks and one of them lifted the box containing the sterling and disappeared out the same door they entered.

Sean and Anton moved to the desk.

Yang stood with his back to them and said, "Hopefully we can meet again in two weeks time, my friends. We need to move as quickly as possible. We can do more damage to America with this weapon than we can with ten nuclear warheads. We can wreck their economy. That's where it hurts the capitalist most. In their big fat wallets."

They split the money up into three bundles. Sean produced two nylon light weight bags from his coat pockets.

They packed eight hundred thousand into each of the two bags which were only meant to hold six hundred and fifty each and Danny and Bobo stuffed another ten bundles of ten grand into their pockets and underwear. Sean pulled out two plastic bags and put one hundred thousand into each of them.

"Here, that's yours," he said as he handed the bags to Anton. This was his share, for among other things, paying off his contacts in the Moscow airport to allow two Irish men free passage through customs and security.

Before they left Sean explained to Yang that if he could not make the next trip, then Danny who was a well trusted and competent officer in the Official IRA would be able to carry on in his place, in any aspect of the operation. Yang was not concerned, he knew within a few minutes of observing him that Danny was a man of honour and inner strength. The other one was different to Yang he seemed to be like a monkey, a monkey who could turn into a dragon and just as quickly back to the happy, funny monkey again.

They left Yang's office and marched up through the long corridor to the security airlock where they had entered.

The four climbed back into the big 4x4 and drove slowly to the gates. Chi followed alongside them and when they reached the gates he went into the small sentry box that operated the gates and housed the CCTV camera images on a bank of monitors. He gave the sentry the nod to open the gate.

As the gates opened Chi stepped out of the sentry box and went to the open driver's window and nodded to Sean in a stiff and respectful manner.

"Goodbye, sir."

Then to the other three Chi said, "Goodbye, comrades. I hope to see you again soon."

Then he made a slight bow. Sean, Anton and Danny made a small gesture of a bow and Bobo tried the full thing almost banging his head of the back of Sean's head rest.

The car left the compound and turned right onto Yamatazara Street. They had only travelled a few yards when a large black car swung in front of them causing Anton to brake.

The passengers were thrown forward in their seats. Danny knew they were being hit. He guessed it was Russian cops. Another car had pulled up tight alongside them. Big, heavy black leather-clad men spilled out of both cars. The first to the driver's door had scars on his scars and eyes that looked like they had witnessed every evil deed imaginable. He got the drop on Anton and had a large revolver pointed at the side of his head.

He yelled in Russian and pulled on the handle of the locked door.

Sean grabbed at Anton's sleeve. "What the fuck?"

"Mafia." Hissed Anton. Sean reached under his seat and pulled out the MAC-10 and held it low to the side of his right knee. The big Russian spat saliva as he yelled at Anton. He yanked at the door handle. Anton sat steady.

His brain was in overdrive. He unlocked the door and shouldered it with his full weight and force. The door knocked the Russian's gun from his grip. He fell backwards onto the road.

Chi had seen what was happening and had sprinted out through the embassy gates, in a flash he was airborne and the ball of his heel hit one of the armed gangsters straight and square on the back of his head. The Gangster went sprawling onto the boot of his own car and walloped his head on the back window. A second gangster to Chi's left was looking at his tumbling side kick and started to turn his face towards the source of his friends down fall the same face in an instant was changed forever as Chi's right fist splattered the nose causing it to explode internally with crushed bone and tissue and externally with fine sprays of blood and mucus.

Anton tried to get out of the Riva. The big gangster jammed the bottom of the car door. He'd recovered his gun and was trying to get a shot off into the Riva. Danny, who had quickly slipped out of the back door behind Anton, landed a sharp Gaelic football kick to the gangster's wrist causing him to fire a shot into his own car. One of the other gangsters from the front car raised a semi auto pistol and levelled it in Danny's direction. Sean let rip with the MAC-10. He fired a short burst at the gangster's feet. The last thing he wanted was a pile of dead Bratva lying outside the embassy and drawing undo attention to his operation.

Danny stalled for a second when Sean fired his burst then continued sinking boot after boot into the first gangster's ribs.

Bobo sat in the car calmly surveying the situation. He wound down the window and poked his head out.

"Kick his ballicks in, Danny!"

The drivers of the two cars got out with their hands held high and Sean kept them covered with his machine pistol. They dragged their wounded and battered Bratva to the cars and sped off, relieved to be escaping with their lives.

Chi ran back to the embassy without saying a word and disappeared behind the closing gates, Danny and Sean jumped back into Anton's car and they sped off.

The whole incident was witnessed by a Russian security agent sitting in the back of an old van parked further down the road. When he radioed in to HQ he was ordered to observe and take notes but take no other action.

Instead of going straight to the hotels Anton detoured to another part of Moscow where he pulled up at a seedy looking bar. A large Armenian man was stood outside and came over to the Jeep. Anton put his window down and spoke to the man in Russian. The authority and urgency in Anton's voice was evident and the man hurried into the bar and emerged a second or two later with five other equally large men who got into two fairly bashed up and rusted Ladas and started to follow them.

Anton stopped first at the Sheraton, and let Danny and Bobo off. They took the two bags of paperwork up to their room and started to pack it into their suitcases which had been left half-empty on the journey over. After going over to one of the Ladas and telling the three men inside to stay at the hotel for Danny and Bobo's protection, Anton signalled to the other Lada to follow him.

They drove to the Metrapol and went to Sean's room. Sean went straight to the bathroom and turned the cold tap on, he threw cold water onto his throbbing face and dabbed it with a hand towel. He came back out and exploded.

"Anton what the fuck, how did this happen. What the fuck! I thought you had this sort of thing covered. Jaysus what a complete balls up".

Anton's anger gave way now to embarrassment. He spoke in a subdued tone.

"I'm sorry Sean, these guys are mavericks, they must have been acting on their own, 'Shpana' they answer to no-one, but they will pay this time".

"No, let it go, as long as we know it won't happen again" said Sean, as his anger ebbed.

"It won't, believe me it won't" Anton replied.

Sean went to the mini bar and took a small bottle of whiskey from it he put it to his head and necked it, they then left to go back to the Sheraton .

Sean was settling the bill at the Sheraton while Anton went upstairs to fetch the boys. He knocked on the room door and Bobo looked through the peep hole.

"It's Mr Can't-get-out-of-the-fuckin-car-big-Russin-spy."

Danny laughed at Bobo's mockery but he knew that Anton was a formidable force and was just unlucky on how things had panned out. The three went down stairs to meet Sean.

Danny looked at Sean and Anton and addressed them both.

"That was a right fuck up today".

Sean replied, "I know Danny I know, Anton is going to sort it".

"I hope so, and I think it would be a good idea that we have a bit more protection on any further trips here".

Anton looked at Danny. "It won't happen again".

"Right let's go," said Sean and moments later they were heading for the airport with Anton's men following.

At the airport they got out of the Jeep and one of Anton's henchmen got out of the Lada and drove off in the Riva after getting instructions from Anton who had earlier phoned Yang at the embassy to tell him firsthand what had happened. He also got a bit of interesting information from Yang. That evening a young Russian electrician who had been working at the embassy was picked up on his way home. The heavy, bulky cell phone he was carrying was used to beat him unconscious and was buried along with him. There are only three types of people who have cell phones in Russia, wealthy business men, high ranking politicians and members of the Bratva, the Russian Mafia. Later that night four known criminals were fired on outside a bar in a seedy side of Moscow, three died at the scene and one escaped.

Sean and Anton waited to board the first flight in a connection that would eventually take them to Birmingham, England. Danny and Bobo would be heading back to Dublin. Their big cases with the blue ribbons tied to them were about to go through the x-ray machine just as the supervisor, a friend of Anton's came up to the machine operator and offered him a cigarette and at the same time asking him what he thought of the previous nights football game. By the time their short conversation ended, the two bags were long gone, and in the hold of the aircraft.

Chapter 4

Mick Rogers picked Danny and Bobo up at Dublin airport.

"Well lads how did it go?" Mick asked as they got into the car. "Not too bad Mick," said Danny. "A wee bit of bother in Moscow but it could have been worse. We had no problem getting the stuff over here, sailed through."

"Aye Sean was on the phone, he didn't say exactly but I got the gist of what happened."

Bobo shouted in from the back. "Aye Mick, I had to throw a few punches to sort it out, ye know like. Danny was useless".

Mick smirked as he looked at Bobo in the rear view mirror, and then looked at Danny who just rolled his eyes.

They went first to the long stay car park where Danny picked up his car. Mick waited until Danny was leaving the car park and then took off for his house with Danny following.

They got to Mick's house in Ashbourne just north west of Dublin, and grabbed the cases and went in. When they got in, they tipped the cases on to the kitchen floor and started to stack the Dollars on to the table.

"There's one point seven mill there, Mick," Danny said.

"Aye I know Sean told me on the phone, he wants you to take one million up North and get a team together and start changing it right away."

"No problem," said Danny. Mick separated the money and he helped Danny pack one mil into one case while Bobo packed their belongings into the other. Mick then put the remaining seven hundred thousand into a large cardboard box and put it up in to the roof space.

Danny and Bobo arrived in Belfast and went straight to one of Danny's safe houses just around the corner from the Workers. Danny carried the suit case in through the front door. The owner of the house just nodded at Danny as he walked past the open door of the lounge. It was all routine. There was one room upstairs for Danny's exclusive use and the owner of the house and his wife never went into that room and didn't want to know what was in it. He rolled back the carpet and stashed the money under the floor boards and went back down to the car. "Right Bobo, what now?"

"What? What now? Round to the club for a decent drink that's what now." Bobo shouted.

Danny left Bobo off at the club and went home to Bronagh.

The next morning Danny arrived at the club and started to clear up and stack shelves. Back to the old routine. Bobo was in behind Danny, almost on top of him.

"Give us a drink there big lad, my mouth tastes like a camels arse."

"Take your time Bobo take your time. Let me get things sorted here first."

Bobo huffed. "Well you can go to Russia on your own the next time ye big shite."

After a short while Bobo had started fidgeting and making impatient noises, but just then Gary walked in to the club.

"Well done, well done muckers. This aul craic might be better than we thought," he said as he slapped Bobo on the back. "I hear you were beating all round you Bobo."

"Oh aye" Bobo said throwing left and right hooks at thin air. Then Gary stopped smiling and his voice became more serious, "Sean was on the phone he told me what happened. You two need to be very careful."

"Yeah I know. Look, Doc", said Danny I didn't mention anything to Bronagh about that bit of a scrap we had so don't say anything to her."

"Okay, but without going behind your back Danny, I'm going to ask Sean to take you off the op."

"Listen to me, Mr Inter-fuckin-feering-father-in-law, I'll decide when to quit, do you think I don't care about Bronagh and the kids?"

Gary put his two hands up in the air and said. "Okay, I'm just worried about you, her and the kids, that's all."

Gary tried to redeem himself. "Do you want a drink there Bobo?"

"Well I don't know. You've kinda upset my best mate here you know. I don't think you should be able to come in here annoying everybody as if you own the place… but, well, well all right, to keep the peace, all right. Just a pint of Guinness and a wee large brandy."

Danny turned round and started pulling the pint and had the brandy poured before Gary could say a word and all the time trying not to laugh.

Gary couldn't think of anything to say he was caught on the hop.

"Put that on my slate," he said to Danny as his face got redder and redder. "And I might not own the place but I'm the fucking manager, okay? Now get this bar cleaned and you Bobo, no more drinking in here before opening time."

Bobo pointed at the clock on the wall behind the bar, "It's one minute past eleven aul hand" and took a long drink out of the pint. Gary turned and walked out of the club, Bobo and Danny did a high five and laughed, and as Bobo went to lift the brandy Danny grabbed it and set it under the bar.

"You can have that later. We've work to do."

At two o'clock that afternoon eight men and six women gathered in another safe house two streets away from the house where the money was stashed. Bobo had gone round the group's homes and places of work telling them about the meeting and had told them to wear their Sunday best, as they would be doing a wee bit of business.

Some of the boys did scrub up well and some generally wore suits from time to time but others only wore suits to weddings and funerals and a few didn't even own a suit, and that's when it did get a bit ridiculous. One of the boys wore a pinstripe business suit which belonged to his cousin who worked for the Civil Service, the brown steel toe cap working boots that still had muck from the building site on them did not do the suit justice. Another one of the guys wore a suit similar to Bobo's white job. Even though it was a better fit than Bobo's the denim shirt just didn't work.

Danny finished his shift early and was about to leave when Bobo walked in.

"They're all round there waiting."

"Okay, we'll go over to the other place to grab the dough."

The pair went to the first safe house and upstairs to Danny's special room. They started pulling the Dollars from under the floor boards and Danny counted out four hundred grand and put it into a big leather holdall. The pair left for the meeting house with Bobo walking ahead of Danny scouting the streets for cops or Brits. They got over to the meeting without incident and went in. Danny pushed his way through the hallway and into the sitting room. The room was packed and thick with tobacco smoke.

Danny started by saying, "Who said you could smoke in here?"

They all answered in unison. "Bobo did."

Danny shot Bobo a look but Bobo just smiled and pulled on his own fag.

"Okay, here's what's happening. As you all know for a while the movement was dealing in counterfeit dollars. We were doing alright for a while, but the quality was not great and one of the lads got scooped and done time. Right, that was then but now we have a completely different ball game here. What we have now is a near perfect note, these notes can only be detected after close examination by experts. Ordinary bank workers can't tell the difference between these and the real thing. Listen lads what we have here are Superdollars."

Danny opened up the holdall and started pulling out the bundles of dollars giving fifty grand to each of the teams.

"Right, transport, how many cars have we got?"

Five hands went up.

"The cars can go to the border to do the change bureaus. Change two and three grand at a time. If you get a young one that looks a bit stupid do four or five. A girl and a fellah in each car. Myself and Bobo will do the border between Newry and Crossmaglen.

Car number one, Forkhill to Monaghan. Second car, Monaghan to Fermanagh. Third car, Fermanagh to Eniskillen. Fourth car, Eniskillen to Derry. Car five can do the banks and travel agents in the shopping centres in Lisburn, Lurgan and Portadown. The thing is we have about three to four weeks before this stuff is discovered so we need to make the most of it while we can. Any questions?"

One of the boys raised his hand.

"Yes?"

"I'll do this job but I'm doing it reluctantly. It smacks too much of criminality, and while we're on the subject when are we going to whack a few of these drug dealers and get them out of our kids faces?"

"Look, as I said, speed is of the essence and when we get as much as we can out of the Superdollar, we'll start to sort out the hoods and druggies."

Another one put his hand up.

"Yes?" Danny asked again.

"I just want to know is it true that Bobo whacked a carpet sales man last week because he heard he was a rug dealer?"

The room erupted in laughter and Bobo shouted over the noise, "I'll whack you, you smartass bastard."

Danny was glad of the bit of banter to lighten the situation. He didn't like trying to justify something he wasn't comfortable with himself.

The motley crew left two at a time and went their different ways, four cars to the border towns, one car to Portadown and the rest made their way by taxi and bus into Belfast city centre to hit the banks and travel agents. Danny told them to meet back at the house at seven o'clock that night.

Danny and Bobo headed down to Newry. The town was full of change bureaus as it was on the main route between Belfast and Dublin. Danny and Bobo worked fast and were able to do in a hundred and fifty K between them. The greedy changers on the Dublin Road were giving out the worst rates in the country and were only to glad to break ten or fifteen grand at a time.

They all got back safe and sound, the border crowd had a mixture of Irish Punts and Sterling as had Danny and Bobo. The boys that done Belfast had got finished in less than two hours and got in touch with Gary and gave him their proceeds. Gary checked the money against the receipts and stashed the cash.

By eight o'clock that evening the money was all in and counted. They had changed four hundred and fifty grand. Danny had told the boys to be back at the house the next day at half ten. He intended doing in the rest of the one million.

Sean was due back from Birmingham on the next evening. He had already done a deal with some contacts of Anton's to move a lot of the dollars on mainland Britain.

The next day things went smoothly again and the remainder of the one million was now sterling and punts. The boys were all brought back to the club for a celebration drink and a bit of a bonus for their work. Danny had told the committee he wanted the back room for a bit of a private get together. Everyone was given a grand each to be used for a holiday or just a bit of a treat. Four of the boys politely declined the offer as it went against their principles. The people who did take the token payment felt a bit uneasy but tried to justify it by declaring how broke they were and sure it was only a few quid compared to the wider picture.

Bobo refused his money too but there were two reasons for that, one was because the smartass who took the Micky out of him had refused his, so Bobo didn't want to let himself down, and secondly, he was afraid he would drink himself to death with that much cash in hand. No he would wait for his fortnightly social security cheque instead.

Sean got back from Birmingham and went straight to Belfast. He met up with Danny, Gary, Jamesy and Finbarr in the back office of the Workers Club.

"Well, lads, things are going well. I am setting things up over in Birmingham with Anton, He's working with a few of the big gangs over there. I'm giving them the dollars at sixty-five cents. I'm doing it to bring the volume up and keep the Koreans happy, and we are still making good money.

With Anton working for us there is no problem, he has a good team over there and none of the other Birmingham gangs will give us any trouble with him and his crowd on our side. I have him and his Russian friends on commission and Anton gets to do an odd deal of his own. So, how have things gone here?"

Sean looked at Finbarr as a matter of formality and respect but the question was really directed at Danny and Gary. Finbarr nodded in Danny's direction.

"Things are going well, Sean. We busted that one mil no problem, and we can go again when you're ready."

Jamesy knew things were going well but was still peeved.

"Listen, this is all going on in Belfast. We should have a say in what's going on." He nodded vaguely in Finbarr's direction as he spoke.

"Listen," Finbarr said. "Sean and the boys are doing all right here. We need this thing to run smoothly so let them carry on, and Jamesy you give them whatever support they need."

Jamesy was about to start his usual screaming match when Finbarr firmly stated.

"That's an order."

Sean, Gary and Danny got up and went out of the office and headed for the exit, leaving poor Finbarr to listen to Jamesy's whinging and whining.

"Right, where's all this dough?" Sean said as they walked out the door. The three got in to Sean's car outside the club and as they pulled away. Another car started up and followed them round to the safe house. They went into the house and up the stairs. The cash was in two bags, one full of Sterling the other Irish Punts. The other car had stopped behind Sean's outside the house. This car was clean, not known to the cops on either side of the border. The driver was a sleeper that Sean used. No one else knew who he was, and when Danny and Gary brought the two bags out to the car and threw them into the boot, he just sat in the driver's seat with his cap pulled down over his face.

"Good luck lads." Sean said as he jumped into his own car.

Sean took off and the sleeper followed. Sean would travel in front all the way down to Ashbourne and he would give the sleeper three flashes of his break lights if there was any trouble ahead. This would allow him time to take evasive action.

Sean, Mick and Cathal met up at Mick's house in Ashbourne.

"So far, so good, Cathal," Sean said. "I've made contact with Anton's crowd in Birmingham. You know to be honest with you Cathal, it makes me sick to have to work with these people. They're scum, but we need to use them to move large volumes of the stuff and keep the Koreans happy."

"I know what you're saying Sean. My mother always said. 'Lie down with dogs and you'll rise with fleas.' But then it's the British system that creates criminals like them and it's that same system that we're fighting here. What about the Belfast boys? How are they getting on? I still have my doubts about Bobo."

"Cathal, Bobo's doing a good job. He knows where to draw the line with the aul messing and drinking. He'll not let us down. And Danny is flying.

I can rely on him to carry on parts of the operation at his own discretion. And I'm going to have to do that. I'm stretched to the limit myself."

"It's just that Jamesy doesn't think they're up to it and he's in Finbarr's ear all the time about them. He reckons he should have more control over things, reckons he has good men up there who could do a better job than Danny."

"Look, Cathal. Jamesy has a bunch of wasters around him. They drink all day and think the movement owes them a living. Most of them have only joined up for protection from the Provos because they got themselves into trouble with them. Look, to keep him quiet I might let Jamesy do a few grand from time to time but I don't think we'll get a good exchange rate."

Sean turned to Mick.

"Okay, Mick. Go and get the other seven hundred K. You've a wee boat trip to take."

Sean made a phone call and around fifteen minutes later the sleeper turned up in his clean car. He had his wife and two kids with him as a cover. Mick said nothing to the driver. He went straight to the boot of the car and put the holdall with the dollars in it below another bag and a child's pushchair. Sean had already spoken to the sleeper and told him what to do. Mick got in beside Sean and they drove off in front of the sleeper to Dublin Port. The same routine, he would flash his brake lights three times if there was trouble ahead.

They got to the Port and the sleeper took his car to reception where he bought a one day return. Just another family going on a day trip to Wales. The sailing was at one thirty. The fast ferry would have them on mainland Britain in two hours. After he got the tickets he drove straight over to the boarding compound and was through security and on the massive catamaran in minutes.

Meanwhile, Sean dropped Mick off as a foot passenger at the reception where he got his tickets -- also a day trip -- and boarded via the foot bridge. It was a nice sailing. The sleeper and his wife had a meal and a drink while the kids ran around the boat and explored. Mick went to the bar and got a pint of Guinness and was surprised at how good it was.

When they got into Holyhead Mick got the shuttle bus that took him out of the port and to the train station. He walked from there to the Breakwater bar a few hundred yards down the promenade. The bar's car park was at the rear and as he walked towards it he could see the red BMW Five series.

Anton was in the front passenger seat and the Birmingham gangster was in the drivers seat. Mick had never met Anton but Sean had given him a good description. He went to the car and got into the back seat. Anton turned around and looked him up and down.

"Mick?"

"Anton?"

He put his hand out and shook with Anton but not with the English crim. There was a small suitcase on the back seat.

"Can I open this?" Mick asked.

Anton shrugged. "If you like. But it is all there."

Mick opened it and gazed at the bundles of sterling in twenties and fifties. He didn't count it. Sean's orders. Mick closed the suitcase. The sleeper's car came into the car park. He got out of the car, along with the wife and kids, he locked the car doors but left the boot unlocked. Then he went into the pub through the back entrance. Mick took the suitcase and went over to the car. He took the dollars from the boot and replaced them with the Sterling. He went back to the BMW and threw the hold-all into the back seat. Anton didn't check it.

The sleeper watched everything from the window seat that he had chosen in the bar. In another ten minutes, he and his family would finish their drinks and take a nice drive along the Anglessy coast before returning in time for the last sailing to Dublin. There were always less security checks on the last sailing.

Mick made his way to the promenade where he found a quiet café and had a few cups of tea. He went for a long walk along the sea front before turning back towards the port to catch the six o'clock sailing.

Sean picked Mick up at Dublin port at eight fifteen and took him back to Ashbourne. Cathal had returned as well after a visit to the clinic for treatment. The aul fellah was on his way out. It was time for him to slow down. But the cause was all he knew from he was a child and he was going to keep fighting for it until his death. Pushing fake dollars was nothing like the military action that he, Sean and others had seen.

The sleeper got back into Dublin at eleven fifteen, no problems. He drove to Mick's house and pulled up in front of the driveway. Sean went out to him.

"All right, Reggie? Everything went well, then?"

"No problem."

Sean looked at his cousin. "Well, Mary, did you have a nice day?"

She smiled at him. "We did surely, you big bollocks. Now give us a few quid and fuck off. And don't expect a kiss either."

Sean winked at his cousin and pulled an envelope from his inside pocket with ten thousand Irish Punts in it.

"Here, Reg. Use some of that to buy her a coat will ye? That one she's wearing looks like shite."

Back in the house, Sean opened up the small suitcase and tipped the money out on to the big dining table. They counted out Anton's Sterling. It wasn't as good as the sort of return they were getting from Danny and the Belfast boys, but it was still good money. Mick brought the cash from Belfast up from one of the bedrooms.

"Right," Cathal said. "Let's keep it simple. We hold on to the Irish Punts, we'll stick half in the bank and keep half for ex's and we will send the Sterling to Moscow. What will we get for it Sean?"

"We'll get around sixteen million dollars. Twenty, if Yang is feeling generous."

Cathal nodded.

"This problem with the Russian Mafia, what was that all about"? He said.

"Anton is sorting that out", said Sean. "Some young guy working in the embassy passed on info to a few low level hoods who didn't know what they were getting involved in. They took it upon themselves to hit us. The young guy has disappeared and three of the gang are dead. The Mafia has assured Anton it won't happen again.

"So what next"? said Cathal.

"I'm going to let Danny go back to Moscaw and set up another deal".

"Danny"? Asked Cathal.

"Yang likes Danny," Sean said. "Trusts him. So Danny can go back over there and do another deal. I have a lot to sort out over here, I need to rein in a few of the units around the country and keep them on board. Danny can handle it, The Mafia are sorted, Anton spoke to them, they said the hit on us was a mistake and it won't happen again".

"What about the three guys that that Anton's mates stiffed? They will hardly let that drop." Said Cathal.

"That's not a problem, that gang were acting without clearance, if Anton hadn't done them they would have got it from their own crowd."

"And the baggage handlers in Moscow airport are they still in our pocket"?

They are still on board, although we do need to watch our backs. It won't be long 'til the yanks start seeing these bills coming in from Ireland and England and they'll start to look for the source. Right, I'll get on to Joxer down in Talbot Street and get a few passports sorted out. I used to think *he* was a bad un until I met these Brit crims."

Cathal frowned and Sean could see he was not completely at ease with the situation, he could see heavy fatigue in his friends eyes. It twanged his heart.

Sean decided to go up to Belfast on Saturday night and let off a bit of steam. When he got there the club was in full swing. A band played in the back lounge and the front bar was packed with punters who seemed to think that prohibition was coming in at midnight. Sean's wife had come along with him for the run and as they entered the club they caught the feelings of festivities and craic. Sean picked a seat for his wife and himself and made his way up to the bar, which wasn't easy as every one of the revellers there wanted to shake his hand and slap him on the back. Sean McStravick -- hero and legend.

Danny served him at the bar. 'Amazing', he thought as he looked at the sweat on Danny's brow and watched him shoot back and fourth across the bar pulling pints, pouring shots, lifting dirty glasses and washing them. And yet, less then a week before, he was kicking the crap out of a Russian gangster and safe guarding a couple of million for the movement.

Belfast *always* amazed Sean and he was quite comfortable to get drunk that night and wake with a mighty hangover the next day in Gary's house.

That song, *The Boys of the Old Brigade*, was still ringing in his head. It had been played four times in his honour, but he could have done without it. Sean's wife Mary and Gary's wife Eileen were downstairs making a traditional Irish breakfast; a grill, better known as an Ulster Fry. They were talking about children and grandchildren and dreams of better lives for everyone.

Gary woke from a nightmare where he watched his beloved daughter clawing at a coffin draped in green white and gold, it contained the riddled body of her dead husband, and Gary wished, he wished, he wished with all his heart and soul that he was not as psychic as his wee granny had told him he was.

Sean finished his breakfast and went with Gary round to the Workers Club. Danny was behind the bar cleaning.

"Well what's the craic, men?"

"How are ye, Danny?" Sean said.

"I'm good."

"I need you to make another trip to Moscow. We're going big. We've enough to pull fifteen mil out, so it's going to be hard going from here in."

"Okay," Danny said. "Um, has Gary filled you in on the Newry job?"

"I haven't yet," Gary said.

"Well what is it, lads?"

Danny cleared his throat. "Right, one of the Newry men, Micky Hijack, has—"

"Micky Hijack?" Sean spluttered.

Gary and Danny shared a smirk.

"It's a well-earned nickname," Danny said. "He used to drive a van for the post office in Newry but every time he was making a money delivery his van happened to get hijacked. The post office couldn't prove a thing against him, so they took him out off the van and stuck him in the sorting office until they can find an excuse to sack him. They couldn't have done a more stupid thing because now we have the whole rundown on every penny going through the place. We can just walk in there and help ourselves to a fortune. I have it set to go on Thursday. They get a pile of money then, to pay out social security payments and child benefit."

Gary huffed through his nose. "Danny, we can make more money with the dollars. Why take risks on robberies?"

"Can't let this one slip by, there could be up to half a million in there. But if it's all right with everyone, I think I'll make this one my last."

Sean agreed to the robbery. The more genuine money they had, the more paperwork they could buy.

Thursday morning, eleven thirty. Derrybeg housing estate, Newry. Danny and Bobo had just put on their postman uniforms supplied by Micky Hijack. Both wore surgical gloves. Danny checked his big Webley revolver and stuck it into his waist band. Bobo had a Glock 17 tucked into his coat pocket.

Bobo looked at Danny and nodded towards the big pistol. "Look at you, Cowboy Joe." Danny adjusted the Webley to make it more comfortable then closed his jacket around it.

"Okay, pardner. Let's go."

One of the Newry men led the pair round to the lockup garage which contained the mocked-up postal van. Bobo got into the driver's side and Danny sat in the passenger seat. They set off.

"Do you know the words of *Moonshadow*, Bobo?"

"Nah, but here's one I do know."

He broke into his own version of *Postman Pat*.

As they drove along the Mall beside Newry Canal they were in fine tune.

"Postman Pat, Postman Pat, Postman Pat ran over his cat!"

They turned left into the back entrance to the post office. No one even noticed them, just another van picking up mail. Bobo reversed the van up to the loading bay and he and Danny got out and climbed the seven steps up to the back door. It was usually kept locked when there was money being sorted, but Micky Hijack saw to it that the door was left open. The two boys walked in and turned right into the main office. A security guard, and two clerks were there.

The security guard bristled. He made a lunge at the pair, arms spread to shunt them back out through the door. He earned himself a whack across the side of the head from Danny's big Webley. Went down like a pole-axed calf.

Bobo pulled the Glock out and pointed it at the two clerks.

"Right men, any of you two hit a button and I start shooting."

Danny dragged the stunned guard over to the radiator and handcuffed him to it. Bobo told the two clerks to open the big wooden cupboards where Micky Hijack had told them the money was kept. After seeing what happened to the guard they almost fell over each other to get the keys and open the doors for Bobo. He looked inside.

"Klondike, big lad! Klondike!"

Danny went over and started to pull the green money bags out of the cupboards and on to the office floor. There were ten of them, each holding fifty grand. There was another twenty thousand on the clerks' desks. Thirty had gone out to the front of the post office where the six tellers had already given most of it out to the unemployed getting their social security cheques cashed and mothers collecting child benefits.

The tellers were soon to experience a sudden shortage of funds and a lot of people in Newry would be rather annoyed at having to wait two or three hours while emergency cash was pulled in from Belfast.

"Right, lads, here's the deal. We can do this the easy way. That is, you both cooperate and we go out and throw these bags into our wee van. We just drive away and you two go back to your office and call an ambulance for the stupid guard, and then you can call the cops, and everything will be sweet.

Then there's the other deal. The one where you two do something stupid and we go to jail so the IRA makes a visit to your houses, where there will be a wailing and a gnashing of teeth and—"

Bobo cut in. "Yeah, and many will be cast into eternal darkness."

Danny threw him a look.

The two clerks dragged three of the bags each out to the van and Danny and Bobo followed with the rest. As they left the office Bobo looked down at the guard, still stunned and nursing a nasty bump on the side of his head.

"Now aren't you sorry you done that? I bet you wish you had stayed in bed this morning."

One of the sorters at the conveyer belt nudged Micky Hijack.

"What's going on over there?"

Micky looked over at the four, dragging the bags to the van and throwing them into the open back doors.

"Looks like we're being robbed. Did you see the game last night? Celtic played well didn't they?"

The sorter frowned. "There was no game on last night."

"Oh?" Micky stared into his face until the dozy aul git got the message and went back to throwing letters and small packages into their designated bags.

Danny and Bobo took the van to a laneway off the Flagstaff road where they abandoned it. One of the Newry men had parked Danny's car there a few minutes before they arrived. They tossed the bags of money into Danny's car boot. His keys were behind the sun visor in the driver's seat. Before Bobo got in, he went to the side of the lane closest to the passenger door. He dropped to his knees and shoved his arm in under a hedge, and dragged out a bottle of petrol with a rag stuck in the top.

He took a lighter from his pocket lit the petrol-soaked rag and threw the Molotov Cocktail hard in through the open back doors of the van. It hit the back of the driver's seat and exploded in a ball of flames. He kicked the doors of the van closed and jumped into the car beside Danny.

They took off, spattering gravel and mud behind them, and were across the border in less than three minutes.

They went to a farmyard not far from a little border town called Carlingford. Reggie waited in an old corrugated iron hay barn, his family car idling as it waited on its cargo. The boys jumped out and threw the money from Danny's car into Reggie's. No one spoke. When the last bag was thrown in, Reggie drove off out of the barn at a leisurely speed and headed for Dublin.

"He doesn't say much, that gringo, does he?" Bobo said.

"C'mon Bobo I'll buy you a pint."

"Ach, I'm not really thirsty. Could we get an ice cream instead?"

Bobo glanced at the shocked look on Danny's face.

"Haaaaa! Caught you there, Cowboy Joe."

Danny shook his head. "Give me your piece. The Newry men will collect it later on and bring it up to Belfast for us."

Bobo handed Danny the Glock and pulled off his gloves. He threw them into a box full of rubbish lying at the door of the barn. Danny put the Glock and the Webley into a plastic box and stuck it under a bale of hay. As he pulled his gloves off, he noticed a small rip on the fore finger of the right glove.

Shit, when did that happen? he thought.

He pulled the plastic box back out from under the hay and wiped it all over with an old rag he'd found on the ground. He held the box with the rag and slipped it back in under the hay. He was worried, when did he tear the glove? Had he left a print anywhere? He dismissed it. *Little chance.* Still, it niggled.

They drove to a bar in Carlingford and played a few games of pool. Danny had a mineral water and Bobo had a couple of pints. They left the bar and drove along the south side of the border. As they went, they made a note of each *bureau de changes* they passed for future reference. They went as far as Monaghan, crossed the border into Armagh and went on to Belfast giving Newry a wide berth.

Danny left Bobo home to have his tea and made arrangements to see him later. He went down to Gary's house. He was told there was a brigade staff meeting on at seven thirty.

Danny arrived five minutes early. Gary had got there ahead of him to attend in his capacity as Finance Officer. Next to arrive was the OC, Finbarr. The Quartermaster and two Intelligence Officers made it soon after. Jamesy Larkin, second in command, the Adjutant, turned up five minutes late.

"Okay," Finbarr said. "We're all here. Now, down to business."

The Quartermaster gave a report on the arms and equipment. All the weaponry was in good working order and well hidden. They had arms dumps that were sealed and safe. They also had weapons close to hand for easy access. Everyone was happy with that.

Intelligence was next on the agenda. They gave a rundown on who they were watching in the areas, their dossiers on the drug dealers and a few possible robberies that Danny could look into. Then a bundle of files were handed to Finbarr that were for his eyes only. Some things were not discussed at routine meetings.

There was no report on training. The Training Officer had been stood down. They had enough trained men to meet their needs. The two lower ranking intelligence officers left, leaving Danny, Gary, Fergal and Jamesy to discuss ongoing operations.

"Well, lads," Finbarr said. "Another good job today. Everything went well then, Danny?"

"No problem. Over half-a-mil sterling and it went straight down to Dublin."

Danny glanced at Jamesy knowing he was angry that the money didn't go to Belfast first so he could get his hands on it. To rub it in, Danny told the meeting how well Bobo had handled things. "It was a brilliant move," said Finbarr "but five hundred and twenty five thousand was serious dough and it's all over the news, the politicians are demanding action, so we better play it low for a while."

Gary gave an account on how the finances stood and how much was being sent to GHQ. The drinking clubs were still bringing in good money and the tax exemption certificate racket on the construction sites was also making good money, but the cert's were starting to get harder to come by and that particular racket would soon be coming to an end. Finbarr, Gary and Danny all agreed that today's robbery should be the last one, for a while at least. Jamesy objected saying that if an opportunity arose they should grab it.

"That's okay," Danny said. "You can do it yourself, then."

Jamesy looked at Finbarr and said, "You see what I mean? I'm getting this insubordination all the time from him and his mates."

"It's not insubordination I'm just pointing out that it's easy to be in favour of armed robbery when you don't have go on the job yourself. And those mates, as you refer to them, are my operatives and they're good men.

They've pulled off good jobs. More than your bunch of clowns have done for the movement."

"That's enough," Finbarr said. He raised his hands to shoulder height. "Now listen. What I say goes here. Danny, all robberies will cease for now. Sean has told me he needs you full time for the dollars thing. So, Jamesy, you can look after any other ops."

"Hold on. I'm suppose to go around kneecapping hoods and collecting money from building sites, while he flies around the world like an executive? I should be in charge of the dollars. He even has that crazy fucker Bobo doing more than my men are doing."

"Look, Jamesy. Sean and Cathal think things are going well enough. Anyway they're going to let you work with some of the next batch that comes in.

Reggie took the post office haul to a different house north of Dublin in Swords. It belonged to a distant relation of his who was on holiday. Mick had seen a few strange cars around his place that looked like Irish Special Branch, so he had phoned Sean and gave him the address. Sean was already there when Mick arrived. He'd gone in through the back door that had been left open for him.

Shortly after Mick arrived, Reggie pulled up. The three of them took the ten bags and the twenty grand into the house between them. They took the bundles of money and started to rip off the post office bands holding them together and replaced them with plain elastic bands. Sean took one hundred K from the pile and put it into a plastic shopping bag to take to the bank. He had been lodging large amounts of cash on behalf of the party for years, so the manager didn't question the transactions. In fact, the manager was glad to see the cash coming in as most of it would be swallowed up by the party's overdraft.

Sean knew that it wouldn't always be as easy to lodge large amounts of money without explanations, so he intended to go to work on the manager and get a few arrangements and understandings put in place.

Another chunk of the robbery haul would go towards other expenses. Printers had to be paid, fuel accounts settled and even their own personal expenses were hard to keep on top of. Running a political party was expensive. They would be back in overdraft in less than a week. The rest of the robbery haul would go towards purchasing more paperwork.

Mick packed bundles of cash into the false bottoms of three suitcases. Danny, Bobo and Sean would take them to Moscow on their next trip, the Koreans liked sterling.

Danny and Bobo arrived at the house in Swords at eight o'clock the following Tuesday. Danny drove the car around the back and went in through the well trundled rear entrance. Mick and Cathal were there along with Sean. Danny noticed the sharp physical decline in Cathal, and although he and Cathal did not always see eye-to-eye, it saddened him to see such a powerful and charismatic man deteriorate so badly. It made Danny aware of his own mortality.

They had both carried in two boxes containing their personal stuff to load into the suitcases with the false bottoms. Bobo had stuck a can of mace pepper spray into his bathroom bag along with his cheap deodorant and shaving cream. After what happened last time he wanted to have some sort of protection. If he couldn't carry a piece at least he had a bit of a deterrent and he wouldn't get jail time if he was caught with it.

"Right, lads," Sean said. "The same again. You two have direct flights to Moscow from the airport here and I'll meet you in the Sheraton tomorrow night at about six, Russian time. Glad to see you got rid of the suit, Bobo."

Bobo was dressed in a less noticeable dark Crombie overcoat and brown cords with a pair of brown Oxford shoes.

"Well, Sean, it seems no one around this set up seems to appreciate good style. And I'd like to point out; I near froze my balls off out there the last time."

Cathal took Sean to the side to give him a few last pieces of advice. Mick took them to the airport, when they got there Mick left the two boys off to go to the gate for their Moscow flight. He drove around the block and returned to departures again to let Sean off to go to his flight to Birmingham where he would meet Anton and fly on to Moscow.

Chapter 5

The flight to Moscow was good for Danny and Bobo. They both slept from time to time and they both had the meal. Danny treated himself to a few beers and was surprised to see that Bobo didn't drink much more than him.

"Are you all right, Bobo? You're a bit quiet on it."

"I'm fine. It's your man four seats up on the other side of the aisle that isn't all right."

"What do you mean?"

"Well, aul hand, he was in the departure lounge in Dublin and he was looking at everyone except us, which means we were the only ones he was interested in. So he's some sort of a cop or one of these hocus pocus spy fuckers that seem to be floating around a lot."

Danny had noticed the spook but didn't say anything. He was just glad that Bobo was starting to get into gear at last.

When they touched down they went to collect their cases and Danny was half expecting the shady guy on the plane to sprint over to them as they lifted the loaded up luggage. He had seen him go through passport control with little difficulty and as Danny watched him go further on, almost out of sight, he took a mental note of the doorway he turned in to. When Danny made it to that doorway it had a sign on it in Russian script and an electronic keypad lock. The spook was probably watching their every move on CCTV.

They lifted their cases and went out of the airport unchallenged. In twenty minutes they were at the Sheraton. Danny gave the taxi driver three notes similar to the ones Cyrus had used the last time and then just before the taxi driver was going to start arguing, Danny took out one more note and held it towards the driver. The look on Danny's face told the driver that was all he was getting and he took it thankfully.

Cyrus was there as usual along with the blonde receptionist. He met them at the entrance and was about to lift their cases when Danny stopped him.

"It's okay," Danny said. He lifted the case himself and Bobo followed suit. Cyrus stood back. He was well used to businessmen who would not let their cases out of their sight. As the two boys left the reception to go to their rooms Bobo shouted to Cyrus.

"Later, big man. Later on, okay?" He nodded and made drinking motions to him.

Cyrus nodded back.

Sean arrived at the Hotel with Anton and went up to the boys' room. Danny let them in. The money was already out of the cases and sitting stacked on the big walnut table in the corner of the room. Bobo sat on one of the beds wearing a luxury bathrobe he had found in the en suite along with a manicure set and various other toiletries. He hacked at his toenails. Little white chips shot everywhere, much to the annoyance of Danny.

"Ok, lads," Sean said. We're going to the Embassy again but we don't have to go through the diplomatic stuff. We'll be going straight in to see Yang."

Anton pulled out the now familiar nylon bags and started to throw the money into them.

"Here, Anton," Bobo said. "If there's any trouble will me and Danny sort it out, or do you think you might get out of the car this time?"

Anton didn't smile. "Maybe I just break your neck for a laugh?"

"Ach. C'mon now. Don't be like that. I'm only slagging you."

Anton flashed his teeth and said, "Yes, I am slagging also, Bobo."

Sean broke the silence. "Right, lads. Let's go. And keep your eyes open." They went to the Embassy in Anton's Riga, Sean pulled the sun visor down so he could watch the road behind him in the vanity mirror. Half way to the hotel Sean piped up.

"A black car's been on us for the last ten minutes, Anton."

"I see them. They are police. I have warned you before, Sean. The police in Russia will move against us when it suits them. The state here is not as friendly now like it used to be. If they have a reason to embarrass the North Koreans for political purposes, they will. Also we need to start thinking of other ways to move the paperwork to Ireland and the UK. My contacts in Moscow Airport are getting nervous."

They arrived at the embassy and went in. They didn't go to see the first secretary this time but went straight to the government agencies department and met with Yang. The greetings were the usual hand shakes and embraces.

"You had trouble the last time, Sean. Our guard could not help you. Our armed personnel can only intervene when the embassy or our people are under threat. Chi did what he could."

"You're right there, Yang," Bobo said. " That aul Kung Fu stuff and all." Wee Chi can fight like fuck"! Bobo smiled and made small Karate chop movements with his right hand. His smile waned as Yang eyeballed him.

"I don't like the use of that word. It is a profanity that America has spread around the world. It has invaded every language and culture, just like their diseases and their false western capitalist philosophy."

Bobo felt scolded.

"I'm sorry about that, Yang." Bobo said in a hang dog manner. Then he chirped up. "Well Yang I can't blame you for hating the Yanks after what they did at No Gun Ri." Bobo had been reading up on Korean history and was trying to use one of the little bits of knowledge he had gleaned to impress Yang.., it worked.

The look of surprise on Yang's face was clear. Danny wasn't sure why Bobo had got such a reaction.

Bobo carried on. "That was one of the biggest atrocities ever carried out by a supposedly civilised nation. The US Seventh Cavalry slaughtered men women and children as they crossed a bridge. It was beside a wee village called No Gun Ri, It's in the Myeon district of Korea."

"Hwangan Myeon district Mr. Bobo," Yang interjected, still impressed.

"Yeah that's it, there were hundreds of refugees moving south there and the US Army just opened fire on them, the officers orders were just this, kill them all. It was so bad that when some of the refugees managed to get under the bridge for protection they had to pile up the dead bodies to form barricades and even then the Yanks called in the Air Force to fly in and open fire over the tops of these human barricades. That went on for three days solid. And America has denied that it ever happened."

Bobo finished and sat back with a serious and smug look on his face that he pointed straight at Danny who just shook his head. It was obvious to him what Bobo had read up on the incident. The only thing is, if Yang had asked Bobo his opinion on anything else to do with Korean history, Bobo would have been lost.

Yang went to the desks at the back of the office the boxes of paperwork had already been delivered. He reached into one of them and took out a jacket. Lifting the bundle of one hundred dollar bills he shook them and declared once again. "This is our weapon, this is our revenge. For No Gun Ri. When the time is right we will strike with our missiles, but in the meantime we will wear them down. We will wear them down."

Back to business.

Yang invited the four over to the boxes to inspect their contents. For the first time Danny noticed MW, which obviously stood for Moscow, printed on the side of the silver grey cartons. He thought it strange that it was English lettering rather than Korean or even Russian. He unhooked the elastic ropes of one of the boxes which held the lid on, and looked in. It was as expected -- one hundred jackets of ten thousand dollars. Sweet.

Yang said, "This may be too much for you to take away at once, but be sure, comrades, it will be here for you when you need it."

Danny's brain had been in overdrive since Anton announced that he had concerns about his contacts at the airport.

"Yang, you have embassies in Bulgaria, Romania and Belarus, places like that. Am I right?"

"Yes, Mr Devine."

"Well, could you move some of the paperwork to, say Romania, where I could arrange to take it on from there?

"We can arrange to deliver the 'paperwork' as you put it, to any of these places. The governments there are quite liberal towards us."

"Well that's perfect. Sean, just a thought, but I think we could organise a few sun worshippers to take a trip to Bulgaria. And later on, around

December, maybe get a few keen skiers to go to Romania on holiday. With a bit of luck' they'll all come home millionaires."

Sean glanced at Yang then nodded.

Bobo had only one thing to say, "Shaken, not stirred, big lad. Eh what?"

They emptied six of the boxes leaving eight untouched. Before they left, Danny asked Yang was there any chance of getting a bit of gear organised for their trips, after what happened with the Bratva. Sean explained that gear meant weaponry.

"Yes, yes, my friends. That is no problem."

Yang opened his desk drawer and pulled out an automatic pistol. He held it up.

"We make this pistol in our country. It is very cheap to produce but still very effective. The TT33 7-62 mm. I will arrange for one or two of these to be placed along with any further deliveries. When you are finished with it and think you are safe, simply dispose of it. There are plenty of rivers and ponds."

He passed the gun to Danny who automatically released the magazine, ejected the round from the breach and caught it in mid air. He looked at both sides of the gun.

"There is no safety catch," Yang said. "We make them cheaper without it. And, my friend, it is not very often we need a safety catch."

Danny balanced the automatic in his hand. "We have a few weapons similar to this at home. The .32 Automatic Colt Pistol. The .32 ACP. They're okay at short range but they've no real stopping power. Not like the Colt 45

Auto. That'll stop an elephant. Still, I'd hate to just throw away a nice wee piece like this."

Danny gave the pistol and clip back and Yang slapped the clip back home with his left hand. He pulled the slide back and released it to carry a round forward into the breach and disappeared the weapon back into the desk drawer. Danny reckoned Yang wouldn't be caught off guard too easily.

As they left his office Yang said, "It is Tae Kwon Do, Mr Bobo."

Bobo looked puzzled.

"Chi is a master of Tae Kwon Do, not Kung Fu."

"Oh right!" Bobo gave Yang the thumbs up then chopped the air a few times with the edge of his hand.

Everything went well on the trip back to the hotels. They went to the Sheraton where Danny and Bobo took five million in paperwork up to their room. Sean and Anton were going to take one mill between them straight to Birmingham. Danny and Bobo would take the other five between them, they didn't need to pack the dollars into the false bottoms of their cases as Anton had told them the baggage handlers in the airport had been boxed off, but this might be the last time he could swing it.

Danny showered and shaved. When he came out of the bathroom Bobo was watching a quiz show on the television. Even though it was all in Russian and he didn't understand one word, he was still glued to the set.

"Right, Bobo. The shower's free now."

"Thank, God. I thought you were going to be in there all night."

Bobo got up from the end of the bed and stretched like a cat, hands high above his head. He blew a long breath.

"I suppose you've used all the hot water."

"It's a hotel. There's loads of hot water."

"Nah, I'm not taking a chance. I'll leave it 'til the morning. C'mon big lad why don't we go out for a walk? A wee dander round Moscow. All we ever see is that aul embassy and this hotel. What do you think?"

Danny thought for a minute. He didn't like leaving the room unoccupied with so much paperwork in it, but he knew security was pretty good in the hotel.

"All right, Bobo. We'll slip out and leave the TV and all the lights on. Just in case."

Danny grabbed a hand full of roubles and pulled his jacket on. Bobo did the same. They went out of the front door so quickly that Cyrus didn't even see them leave. They had a stroll around the Rameskin district and stopped for a drink in a few of the small pavement cafes. Sipped a few coffees and Bobo contented himself with just one wee vodka. Danny thought the whole Bratva ambush had spooked Bobo enough to slow down his reckless side.

After a while they decided to go back to the hotel. They where both tired and relaxed after their pleasant evening. They cut through a side street, they had worked out that it would bring them back to Yamskaya St and into the hotel. They were halfway down the street when a familiar figure stepped out of a dark little bar/café. The massive size of the man and the black leather jacket alerted them right away as to who it was.

"Suffering duck. It's the big cunt who tried to rob us, Dee-Dee."

Bobo whipped his head from left to right, trying to work out the best way to handle the situation. Danny could see the gangster still had traces of a black eye and a sticking plaster on the left side of his forehead. He remembered the moment his boot connected with the gangster's head that day. The leather-clad ogre had just turned on the pavement and had walked five paces towards them before he visibly started. His look sharpened in recognition. The ogre stalled for a second and seemed to grow bigger in bulk and height as he stared at Danny.

"You. You. I kill you. I break your skinny neck in half."

The ogre lumbered towards them. Danny tried to work out his best move. The Russian was twice his size and although there were two of them against one Russian, Bobo wasn't exactly Muhammad Ali. He scoured the ground for a brick, a plank of wood, anything at all.

The Bratva loomed. His massive hands were wide open and just about level with Danny's chest. Bobo stepped forward, shoulder-to-shoulder with Danny. He raised his right hand and pointed it at the big Russian,

"Take that," Bobo said. His tone dripped with authority. Bobo had taken charge.

He pressed down on the nozzle of his can of mace not knowing he was holding it sideways. A jet of the blinding fluid squirted out and straight across Danny's right eye, it stung like it'd been lanced with a red hot needle. Just outside his world of pain, Danny heard Bobo curse at the mace canister as he looked at it accusingly. The Russian grabbed Danny in a bear hug and wrestled him to the ground. Danny landed on his back. Air blasted from his lungs. The Russian crushed down on him. Danny snaked his right arm across the gangster's chest and fought in vain for some breathing room. Danny growled.

"Bobo, do something for fuck's sake. *Do something.*"

Danny, half-blind, worked his forearm against the Russian's throat. The monster continued to push his face towards Danny. The big Ivan gnashed his teeth inches from Danny's face. The smell of his breath was putrid. A mixture of garlic, tobacco, and cheap vodka. It wasn't the last thing Danny wanted to smell before his nose was bitten off. Danny screamed.

"Jesus, Bobo. Where are you?"

The pressure on Danny's chest eased slightly. The big fucker wriggled about. Danny guessed Bobo was finally trying to intervene. He could just about make out Bobo's form hopping about above them.

"Bobo, Jesus Christ, will you do something."

"I can't get a clear shot at his eyes," Then Bobo asked in a casual manner. Here Danny, do you think mace works on ears?"

Danny screamed. "Fuck ye Bobo Fuck ye. Fuck ye, just do it."

"Oh right, dead on. Now don't be getting too excited there big lad"

Danny heard a hiss and a wet splatter. The weight disappeared from his chest. He could just about focus on the big gangster standing with a hand cupped on his right ear. He didn't scream.

"It doesn't work on ears, Danny."

Bobo skipped forward and loosed another stream of mace into the Russian's bulging eyes. The big lump dropped to his knees. He clawed at his eyes.

Danny struggled to his feet. The sting in his right eye flared anew. His battered body fought through an adrenaline plunge to keep him upright. He felt Bobo's hands on his back.

"Steady, there, Danny. Your work's not done yet."

Bobo gently pushed him towards the kneeling Russian.

"Right, here we go, mucker," Bobo said. "That's lovely. Just swing a wee right hook about body height, there."

Danny could just about make out the outline of his foe's head. He squeezed his fist into a hammer and drew his shoulder back about four inches to give him enough room to send his fist, forearm and triceps on a bone-crushing collision course.

Danny's right fist connected to the left side of the Big six foot six, twenty two stone Russian's face, which looked like it was made of granite, but it wasn't, and as Danny's fist made contact that fist did not give way, it travelled onward pushing flesh against teeth roots and cheek bone which started to crack and break, the hinge which held the jaw bone to the skull buckled from the whiplash effect causing irreparable damage as it gave way to the intruder which was Danny's fist.

Any slower, with less energy and force behind the punch may have given the Russians face enough resistance to maybe withstand it a little, just enough for a small fracture to occur in one of Danny's knuckles or maybe the wrist would have folded a little to lessen the force and the velocity, but no, no, straight through, and the Big Russian Mafia tough guy was going to spend the rest of his life sucking his meals through a straw, the liquid meals that his mother would prepare for him in their run down little shack in a small Armenian village, you see there isn't an awful lot of opportunity to move forward in the Bratva when you get your ass kicked so badly, especially when it happens twice in a matter of weeks.

By the time they got back to their hotel, Danny was starting to recover. He couldn't have been much to look at, though. Cyrus intercepted them at the hotel door, his face creased in concern.

"What happened?"

"Ah it's nothing he just got something in his eye. Bobo said.

Danny fixed his good eye on Bobo. Made it clear that he wanted to throttle him. Then they made a beeline for the bar. Bobo sloped off to check the room.

Danny ordered a large brandy and had set up a pint of Guinness for Bobo. The wee torture arrived back minutes later.

"Ah, great stuff, big fellah. Great stuff. This is my scene now."

Bobo hopped up onto the barstool beside Danny like a child would climb up onto a hobby horse on a carousel. He grabbed hold of his pint and swallowed three quarters of it. Then he plonked it back down on the bar and leaned back on the big bar stool.

"Lovely." He wiped the froth on his upper lip with the back of his hand. "I love a good pint after I've been fighting."

Danny spluttered into his brandy. He turned to slap Bobo's head but stopped when he clocked the big smile on Bobo's face. He could do nothing more than laugh.

"What the hell was that earlier, Bobo?"

"What?"

"That 'suffering duck' shite. What were you on about?"

"Oh. Well, you see, since Yang told me off, I've decided not to use the eff word anymore. And you see, my ma, well my ma was fairly good living. She never liked to use the eff word either. So she used to shout suffering duck, before she hit you with the floor brush."

"Well you could have picked a better time to change your vocabulary. You distracted me."

Bobo gave him a blank look.

"Anyway," Danny said. "We'll have a drink tonight. I phoned Sean and he told me it was all right. He has a few of Anton's men outside in case of any fall out from tonight's wee skirmish."

"Great steam, big lad. Great steam. Here, I've wanted to do this for weeks. I'll order the drinks." Bobo waved the barman over.

"Yes, sir. What can I get you?"

"I'll have two Vodka Martinis. And here, I want them shaken, not stirred."

Relaxed and safe, Danny and Bobo tore at it. Cyrus joined in. Danny switched to pints of beer and Bobo to Guinness. Cyrus was on his usual, vodka and water. The bar was quiet with a bunch of middle aged Russian couples sat at the window tables of the lounge, and a few others punters scattered about. As the night went on and the drink started to kick in Danny got a bit quiet with an air of melancholy about him, so Bobo decided to cheer him up, he got the background music turned up and tuned in to something more lively and treated the other patrons to an odd mixture of a Michael Jackson routine blended with a few steps of Irish Dancing. Danny gave him a few seconds to lap up the applause then told him to sit down.

It got late. The blonde receptionist had finished for the evening and the night porter took over behind the bar. She had phoned a friend.

"Can we join you three?" the receptionist asked.

Her phoned friend was with her. Great tits!

"No problem," Bobo said. "Sit down, sit down." He stood up to make room for them and almost fell into the dark-haired girl's massive cleavage.

"We are very relaxed here tonight, no?" Cyrus said.

The receptionist's friend began speaking in Russian.

"Please, Allyona" Cyrus said. "Our visitors would like it if we spoke in English."

"Aren't you worried you'll be fired, Cyrus?" Allyona asked.

"The fat cat is away. Cyrus will play."

"What fat cat?" Danny asked.

The receptionist smiled at him. "Our boss. He would have an attack in his heart if he knew that we were entertaining bad boys like you and your little friend."

Bobo held his glass over his crotch. "I'm not feeling too little right now."

Danny was drunk enough to flash Bobo a wee grin. In fact, a few more beers and he might even sit a little closer to the receptionist.

Bobo grinned and nodded at Cyrus' back as the big lump staggered off towards the back room behind the reception desk. Looked like the night porter was losing his camp bed for the night again. His mind quickly returned to Allyona and her massive boobs. Then his head turned. No point in thinking about them when they were right under his nose. He wondered how far they would fall if he got to whip her bra off.

The night porter coughed and glanced at his watch. Bobo reckoned they'd be hard pressed to get any more drink from the sour wee prick. He thought for a second.

"Let's go up to our room for a few more drinks," he said. See there's a mini bar up there."

Danny gave him that big sensible look, but the girls were on for it. On the way past the reception Blondie went behind the desk and lifted a set of keys. In the lift, Bobo sidled up to Allyona and put a hand on the small of her back.

May as well be hung for a sheep as a lamb.

He traced the line of her spine with his fingertips. Came to rest on the top of her nice little pear-shaped bum. He thought, *if she pulls away then I'm just wasting good drinking time with a flirt. But if not...* She grabbed a handful of Bobo's arse. Almost broke his tailbone. Bobo gave this development some consideration and decided, he might on to a good thing.

The lift reached the boys' floor and the doors hissed open. They shuffled out into the corridor. Allyona said something to Blondie and took the key from her. Three doors down from the boys' room, Allyona hooked an arm around Bobo's and slipped the key into the door of the unoccupied room. She winked at Bobo and led him in. Bobo looked over his shoulder at a stunned-looking Danny.

"See you in the morning big lad and don't forget to rubber up!" Then he slammed the door in Danny's face.

Danny and the blonde receptionist stopped at the door of his room. She stepped towards him, wrapped her arms around his neck and pulled him towards her kiss. Danny's muzzy mind was still in its nostalgic mode and hadn't even seen it coming. He let the kiss happen for a few seconds longer than he should have then pulled back. She looked at him with a frown and a mixture of surprise, disappointment and indignation. She'd the look of a girl who'd never been rejected before. Danny took her wrists and gently pulled them down in front of him. He shook his head.

"I'm sorry but no. I'm married." He pointed at his wedding band. "Sorry."

She sneered a little and said, "She must be very special."

"Yeah. Yeah, she is."

Lucky for Bobo, and even more so for Allyona, Bobo *had* showered that day. It was close enough to six weeks since his last one, so he thought why not go at it in style?

The girl stepped out of her dress and closed in on him. The main question on Bobo's mind that night was about to be answered. He unhooked her bra. They hardly moved.

Bobo had been divorced for longer than he cared to remember and his sexual exploits in the last two years amounted to a knee trembler at the back of the Shamrock Bar in Santa Ponsa. The girl on the receiving end of Bobo's passion was even more drunk than he was but he still remembered how, when he unhooked her bra, everything went south. Her nipples were closer to her toes than they were to her chin.

But that had been two years ago, so no chance of brewers droop with a vision like Allyona in front of him. He hurried her to the bed.

Bobo woke the next morning with his tongue stuck to the roof of his mouth, a sore dick and an empty mini bar in a room that wasn't his. Life had never treated him more kindly. He looked over at the girl in the bed beside him and wished he could bring her back to the Workers Club just to show her off, and tell everyone how much she adored him and his fine body. As he got up and started to grab his clothes together she woke. She smiled at him

"Hi, Bobo." The greeting sounded lovely in her Georgian accent. He'd discovered during the night she was from Georgia. Somewhere in the south, according to her.

"Well, what about you, love? Good aul night then, wasn't it."

"Ah, Bobo. Come back to bed."

"Sorry there, mucker. Bit of business to take care of, ye know? Shaken, not stirred and all that craic."

She didn't seem to get the joke. Bobo shrugged. Oh God what a great shag she had been.

"Bobo, I will see you again soon?"

"No problem, kid. No problem."

She shrugged and cupped her ear.

Bobo spoke more slowly and louder. "I will see you next time I come back."

He illustrated the point with a bunch of improvised Red Indian signs of Great Eagles flying off and returning. She grabbed him by the shoulder and pulled him down for a farewell kiss that made his toes curl. He pulled away from her.

"Bobo. Why do they call you this name, Bobo?"

"Where I come from in Ireland, it means *Mighty Warrior*." He clenched his fist and held it to his breast and stared at the ceiling. Then he looked down at her on the bed and thought, *I wish I could bring you back to Belfast.*

Danny was up and showered but still feeling rough when Bobo started to bang on the door.

"Jesus, Bobo take it easy," He said as he let him in.

"All right, Danny Dee? All right, kid?" Bobo slapped him on the shoulder and sauntered past him. Then he stopped in his tracks as he surveyed the scene in front of him. One bed slept in and hardly even disturbed and the little disturbance there was happened to be on one side only.

"Suffering duck, now what the hell is this Danny Dee? What's going on here? Do I have to go back to Belfast and tell everybody that Danny Devine is now a born again virgin?"

Danny had pulled the suitcases out from the wardrobes and started to pile his personal belongings into one of them and nodded to Bobo to do the same with his. Bobo started to pick things from around the room and throw them into his case. He butchered the vocal track to *Like a Virgin*, while he worked.

Danny turned and made a dive for Bobo. The wee man had been expecting it and ran round the other side of the bed. He grabbed his crotch and whooped.

"All right, Bobo. After ten years of trying, you finally got a shag. Well, when I get back to Belfast everybody will hear, that after the second blowjob Bobo slipped his hand down her knickers and found a bigger cock than his own." "Ah now, hold on a minute there, Danny. Like, that sort of thing can take on a life of its own. Let's talk this over like adults, now c'mon."

Danny waved him away. Game set and match, Danny had won.

They packed their bags and waited for Sean's call.

Danny and Bobo went down to the lobby with their bags. Sean and Anton met them with their tickets and instructions. Breakfast was out of the question. Anton was smiling, he had got reports back from his men on how the evening had gone. Anton wished he could have a night like that, to have that fun, but at this time it was impossible. In Russia he lived on the edge. Maybe some day when he had made enough money he would be able to go and live somewhere safe, somewhere where he could sing, dance, get drunk and screw models in a top class hotel without the fear of an assassin's bullet in the back of his head.

Anton drove them to the airport with his black leather minders travelling behind in their old Lada. It was hard to tell the difference between Anton's ex-KGB men and the Russian Mafia, but Anton knew the faces. They got to the airport and split up, they had been followed by Russian Secret Service, but not accosted or detained by them. Anton was right. They would not intervene until it was politically advantageous to do so. In the airport they split up as usual, Danny and Bobo to Dublin and Sean and Anton to Birmingham.

Anton's contacts in the baggage handlers did their stuff. Danny and Bobo didn't say much during the flight. They were both nursing massive hangovers. Bobo still managed a few beers but Danny stuck to mineral water.

Chapter 6

Danny and Bobo got in to Dublin and were met outside the terminal by Mick Rogers.

"Well boys. Everything go all right?"

"No problems, Mick," Danny said. "Where are we going?"

"Just up the road a bit. To the Swords house."

"Thank God, do you know if there is any Alka Seltser there?"

"I'm sure we can get you something."

They got to the house in Swords. Mick, feeling sorry for Danny, went straight to one of the kitchen cupboards, and found a box of dissolvable tablets. Danny snatched them from him and went to the sink. He lifted a glass and half filled it with water without even checking if it was clean or dirty. He ripped open four little foil sachets and dropped the eight tablets into the glass.

Mick lifted the empty box and read out loud. "Take two tablets dissolved in water."

Danny ignored the attempt at medical advice and raised the glass to his lips.

Mick's eyes bulged. "Jaysus, Danny. Don't drink that. You'll kill yourself."

The cloudy water and half dissolved tablets went down Danny's neck. He relished the taste of the chemicals and belched.

Bobo's head emerged from the fridge, a can of Guinness in each hand. "Alka Seltzer, my ballicks. This is the gear." Both were opened and both were downed in less than a minute.

"Right, Mick" Danny said. "Here we go."

Danny and Bobo emptied there cases onto the kitchen floor. They started to separate the dollars from the rest of the contents and stacked them in neat piles.

"Five hundred jackets," Danny said.

Mick slapped one of the jackets against the palm of his hand. "Nice."

Bobo tugged at Mick's sleeve. "Any more Guinness?"

"Sorry, Bobo. But here, let's celebrate in style."

Mick went to the medicine cupboard and took out a bottle of Black Bush. He poured three glasses. Danny took hold of his and sniffed it. The aroma of the classic whiskey invaded his nostrils and his stomach turned somersaults. He ran to the toilet in the little utility room beside the kitchen and bent over the bowl.

"Ralf. Huey!" Bobo sniggered and lifted his whiskey.

They split the dollars up. Two hundred jackets went up into the roof space and three went back into one of the cases.Mick drove Danny and Bobo to their car and they were on their way to Belfast with the three mill.

They got to the Lower Falls unhindered in just over two and a half hours and went to the club where Gary was waiting.

"Well lads how did it go?"

"Dead on," Danny said. He held up the case and said "Three hundred jackets in here."

Gary took the three million and threw it behind the bar like it was the weeks washing.

"Right who wants a drink?"

"Nah, I'm all right," Bobo said.

Gary took his eye off the pint of Guinness he'd already started to pour for him and studied the serious look on Bobo's face. Bobo winked.

"Hah. Caught you there, Doc. Wise up, eh? I'd drink it out of a piss pot."

Gary rolled his eyes and asked Danny.

"Just a Coke for me."

Gary put up the Coke and pulled himself a pint of beer while Bobo's Guinness settled. He rang it into the till and patted his pockets for the money.

"I'll pay for this, Gary," Bobo said.

Danny turned on his stool to look at him. Bobo pulled a one hundred dollar bill out of his pocket and slapped it down on the counter. He sat back on the bar stool with a grin. Gary and Danny looked at him and then looked at each other. Danny rushed Bobo and dragged him off the bar stool. Gary came out from behind the bar. He grabbed one of Bobo's ankles and Danny got the other. They hauled him upside down and shook him.

"Come on," Danny said. "Where's the rest?"

A few lose coins, a cigarette lighter and a set of rosary beads fell out of his pockets.

Blood rushed to Bobo's head and his face blazed red. He wriggled like a snared rabbit. "It was just a joke. I haven't got any more."

They dropped him on to the bar floor and returned to their drinks. Bobo sat up and rubbed his battered elbows and knees.

"Suffering duck. Can you two not take a joke?"

"Yeah, it's all right joking," Danny pointed at the suit case behind the bar. "But there's one of those jackets in there that's one hundred short."

"Well I'm not stupid. I marked the jacket. Look and see. You'll find one with a bill folded down."

Gary went behind the bar, he opened the case and found the marked jacket. He lifted it up and showed it to Danny.

"Here it is."

He shoved Bobo's note back into the band.

Danny turned around to tell Bobo it wasn't such a bad a joke after all and spotted him zipping up his fly. A puddle of piss spread out over the floor of the lounge.

"There. Yeh can clean that up yeh smart bastards." Then he bolted for the door.

Danny phoned Bobo the next day. They declared a truce to speed up a return to more serious matters. There was to be no more fooling about. Bobo agreed and said he would be down in the club in half an hour.

Bobo took Danny's word with a pinch of salt. He put on old clothes because he expected that some where between his house and the front door of the club, Danny and Doc would be hiding in wait with the bucket of soapy water that they'd mopped the piss up with. It was standard procedure, but the trick was to wear old cloths and when you see it coming just turn and take it across your back. Last thing you'd want was a face full of the pissy water – or worse again, a mouthful.

The ambush didn't happen, much to Bobo's surprised relief. He walked into the club and found out exactly why the truce stuck. Sean

McStravick was at the bar. The boys knew that things looked like they were going to go back to the old ways, when discipline and careful planning was the order of the day.

"Right, Danny," Sean said. "I'm going to Belarus to team up with another contact so we can move some of the paperwork from there by road. There's a guy I know, he has a haulage firm and he's drawing timber from Belarus to the UK for the next few months. I think we can work with him. I want you, Bobo and Gary to do another trip to Russia. Anton reckons he can get one more run through the baggage handlers, so we need to make the most of it."

"No problem," Danny said.

Gary smirked at Bobo. Looked like he was well up for the trip. Sean gave Danny a briefcase with money, tickets and confirmation of their hotel rooms. Bobo laughed at the sight of Danny with a briefcase.

"There's a false passport in there too, Danny," Sean said. "I've had word from the Koreans that the American security services are going to home in on us soon."

Danny flew out on his own the day before Bobo and Gary. Bobo had openly huffed about the fact that Danny was booked into the Metropol this time while he and Gary had to slum it in the Sheraton. When Danny got to the Moscow Metropol, he unpacked and showered. He changed and made use of the coffee making facilities in the room and relaxed. It was so peaceful without Bobo. He wished Bronagh was with him.

At the airport Bobo took charge. Even though Gary was his superior, Bobo felt he was the main man on this trip and directed Gary around the airport. He told him what to do and when to do it. He also provided a running commentary on the different countries they were flying over. Gary actually seemed to appreciate it. With Danny it was usually, "Shut up, Bobo," and, "Go to sleep, Bobo."

Danny had worked out the approximate time Bobo and Gary would arrive and he made his way round to the Sheraton. He sat in the reception area in a corner. The outer wall was glass from ceiling to floor and everything that was going on in the street could be seen. The barman had already brought him a bottle of water. He didn't have long to wait. He could see the taxi pull up outside and watched as Bobo and Gary got out. The driver went to the boot to pull the large cases out. Not knowing they were almost empty, he almost twisted his back as he braced himself to pull out what he thought would be heavy cases, and almost fell back on to the ground. He sat the bags down on the pavement and turned to Bobo.

Danny watched what seemed like an old black and white silent movie. The taxi driver left the cases on the pavement and aimed a few words at the ploughed field that was Bobo's worried face. Then Bobo shrugged shoulders and reluctantly pulled out some of the roubles that Danny had given him. He held them in front of him with both hands. Then as the taxi man reached out for the cash. Bobo pulled back and half turned his body to shield the roubles from the grasp of the driver. Then Bobo turned back to face the driver and peeled off about seventy-five pence worth of roubles to reluctantly hand to the driver who, by this time had lost his patience and a good part of his mind. The driver grabbed at Bobo's hands to retrieve what he truly believed was a just fare for his drive from the airport.

Danny got up from his comfortable seat, waved to Cyrus and nodded in the direction of the door. Before either of them made it to the door, Danny caught the end of the silent movie through the window as Bobo's forehead smashed into the bridge of the taxi driver's nose. Gary looked around eyes like headlights. His mouth worked but no words left his lips. The taxi driver crumpled to the ground. His nose poured crimson onto the footpath.

Cyrus stepped around Danny and went over to the screaming and cursing driver. He lifted him up from his knees to his feet and then produced a large white handkerchief to help stifle the blood. Cyrus led the taxi man into the foyer and directed him to the restrooms to clean him up.

A few minutes later, Cyrus returned with the slightly calmer taxi man. He nodded to Danny and advised him to pay the driver the three thousand roubles which was the proper fare from the airport, and he suggested a fairly decent tip. Danny was happy to pay up. The disgruntled taxi driver peeled a damp paper towel from his face and delivered a barrage of aggressive Russian in Bobo's direction. Bobo stepped up to fighting range and swung a low roundhouse kick at the driver's stomach. Unlike the previous perfect head butt, Bobo's kick missed its target and travelled on a little further, just enough to find Gary's crotch.

Danny and Bobo helped Gary into the reception and sat him down on one of the big ultra comfortable couches.

Gary babbled to himself. "Why am I not in Belfast, safe and sound in the Workers Club? All you have to worry about is some Provo with a grudge coming in and letting loose at you with a few bursts of an Armalite. Or a Loyalist death squad planting a booby trap bomb under your car. At least you know where you stand there. Two minutes in this country and I'm going to have to watch my back for machete-wielding taxi drivers."

Cyrus was assured that there would be no more kicking or head butting and everyone settled down. Gary was sent to his room to relax. Danny took Bobo to the bar. He allowed himself a pint. Cyrus refused a drink as he was still on duty. After a few pints, Danny convinced Gary to join Bobo at the bar and left a little happier in the knowledge that somebody was looking after the wee rocket.

After Danny left, Bobo felt like he could relax. Cyrus who had just finished work for the evening joined Bobo and Gary for some serious drinking. While Cyrus kept Gary company, Bobo staggered over to the blonde receptionist. He wanted to know where his goddess was.

"Can you not phone her?"

"I am sorry, Bobo. She has gone home for a few weeks."

"Ah, suffering duck."

Bobo's shoulders drooped forward. He'd really wanted to show her off to Gary.

Next morning Anton met Danny at the Metropol and took him to the embassy to meet Yang. They transferred the paperwork from ten of the boxes into bags to take to the hotels. The three Belfast boys had room in their big cases for three mil each and Anton was going to Birmingham with the remaining one. There were two car loads of Anton's men waiting to escort them and the money on their journey to the hotels and then to the airport.

This was the biggest single move yet and Danny had insisted on Anton taking extra help. He didn't care what it cost; Danny didn't want anything to go wrong on his watch. Besides, the money that Anton's men worked for was a pittance, although they where glad of it, since Putin came to power and dismantled and reconstructed the Security Services they had been left out on a limb.

Gary could not believe how cool and calm Danny and Bobo were in this situation, they were handling millions of dollars like they were packets of wine gums. And the fact they were doing it in Russia seemed like nothing unusual. He started filling his case along with the two boys who were chatting and making small talk as they packed.

The three amigos got back to Dublin without any difficulty and again were met by Mick Rogers who took them to Swords. Half the paperwork was left in the house in Swords then Reggie showed up and they put the rest into his car. They set of for Belfast with Danny driving in front as scout. When they arrived in to Belfast they threw everything into one house and after Reggie left they split it up into three and stashed it in three different safe houses. To Danny it seemed the place was awash with dollars. *How in the name of God am I going to move all of this?* He thought. But he did.

Between the boys going round the change bureaus on the border and Sean and Anton's set up in Birmingham, the money was changed into Sterling and Punts like wildfire.

Sean came back from Birmingham and arranged to meet up with Danny and Gary. For security reasons they met in a hotel in the centre of Belfast. Sean was starting to get a lot more careful about how things were being done.

Well lads I'm getting rumblings from my contacts in the Irish Special Branch, now I know we are shifting a lot of stuff, but I would like us to move even faster.

Any suggestions?"

"I'll tell you what. Sean." Danny said. "There is about ten to fifteen of our boys living in London. They're working on the building sites and they would be game enough to do a few grand in for us over there. In fact Bobo told me some of them drink in a bar in North London, they actually call it the Gangsters because of the dodgy guys that drink in it, there could be something there. Bobo has two brothers working over there they have a flat in Wood Green, the rest of the boys are over on the Holloway Road so it would be safe enough to use the Wood Green gaff as a base."

"Well if you think you can work something over there then go ahead. When can you start?" Sean asked.

"Any time Sean." Danny said. "I've already discussed it with Bobo and he reckons there's no problem, he's been over there a lot in the past few years and he knows his way around. I'll send him over with half a mill first and see how he gets on.

Gary spoke for the first time. "I can't believe the way Bobo is handling all this craic, he's taken to it like a duck to water."

"Bobo never surprises me." Sean said.
"By the way, Danny, when you send Bobo to London for Jaysus sake don't let him wear that fecking white suit."

Danny told Bobo what had been decided and told him to start moving some of the paperwork over to London, so Bobo hired a car for a week. He used a firm that stocked English reg' cars as he didn't want to be driving around London in a Northern Ireland registered car and getting pulled in by police every ten minutes.

He went to the Ferry Terminal in Larne and bought a five day return. The fast ferry arrived in Stranraer Scotland after a two and a half hour journey. Bobo was soon on his way along Mad Mick's mile, so named because of the crazy Irish lorry drivers who constantly thundered down it on their way to London and the continent. He drove for five hours and stopped at Watford Gap Services and booked into the little Premier Inn Hotel where he had a meal and surprised himself by only drinking two glasses of wine before hitting the sack. Maybe he was taking this job too seriously. He got up the next morning and was in London in two hours.

Bobo found his way to the flat in Wood Green. He rang the bell for flat three. A few minutes later he heard the lock on the door turning. He expected Tony or Mark to answer. As the door opened Bobo put his arms out to present himself to his siblings.

"What about youse? WOAH!"

Bobo jumped back in surprise at the black face of the Ghanian student who appeared in the doorway.

"Oh, sorry, mate. I was looking for my brothers."

"The Paddies? They are in number two. They moved downstairs."

"Tony and Mark, not Paddy!" Bobo said, and muttered a racist remark.

Bobo banged on the door of the right flat. This time the door was answered by a half asleep Mark.

"Well, how's it going? Come in."

The flat was a tip. Dirty plates, carryout boxes, and empty beer bottles lay about. *Ah, just like home*, Bobo thought.

"Where's Tony, Mark?"

"He's away to work."

"Why are you not at work?"

"I took the day off to wait on you."

"Why didn't Tony wait?"

"Because…"

"Yeah, because you're a lazy big shite."

"Listen to you. You haven't worked since you left school."

"I hurt my hand didn't I?"

"That was eighteen years ago."

"All right, all right. Never mind. Give me a hand with my cases."

They both went out to the hire car.

"Where did you get that?" Mark said as he looked at the brand new Vauxhall.

"It's hired."

Bobo opened the boot and pulled the two suitcases out. They carried one each up to the flat and threw them down on the floor. Bobo told Mark to get dressed to go out. He wanted to go down to the building site where Tony was working.

"You got a bag, Mark?"

Mark searched out a holdall that he used for his weekend trips back home. Bobo lifted one of the cases and set it on the old kitchen table in the middle of the flat. He opened it up.

"Holy fuck," Mark said. He gawped at the case full of hundred dollar bills.

"I don't like that word, Mark. It's a profanity, spread throughout the world by the Yanks. *I* don't use it anymore."

Mark never heard a word Bobo said. "I'll never have to work again."

"That's Sticky money, Mark."

"Fuck's sake." Mark said in disappointment.

"Cheer up, you lazy shite. You might get a couple of good nights out. Maybe a week's wages out of it. But that's all, right? So keep your hands off it."

"Do you think I'm stupid? I like my kneecaps where they are."

"Mark, something this big, you're more likely to get one behind the ear."

"Ha listen to you, Bobo. When'd you get so serious?" He nodded towards a shabby settee in the living room area. "You can sleep on that."

Bobo puffed his chest. "I don't think so."

"Well you're not sleeping in my bed."

"None of us are sleeping here tonight, grab a toothbrush."

They left the flat and walked over to the underground station. Bobo had taken fifty K from one of the suitcases and the fake passport Sean had given him.

He put the suitcases into a cupboard and covered them in dirty clothes and bed linen. *No one will go near this*, he thought. He made sure the skid marks on the sheets were well visible.

They took the Piccadilly Line down to Leicester Square they got off and strolled towards Piccadilly Circus to the construction site where Tony worked. Bobo got to work right away, he couldn't believe the amount of change bureaus there were. He sneaked two jackets out of the bag and told Mark to stand about twenty feet away and watch out for cops and pickpockets. Then he went to the glass screen, looked at the tourist rates being offered.

That's criminal, he thought.

He slipped the two thousand dollars and the passport into the stainless steel drawer. The cashier slid the lid forward and took them. Without even a glance at Bobo she counted out twelve hundred and twenty GBP. Bobo lifted the money and passport from the drawer and stuck them into his coat pocket. He scooted back to Mark.

"Right, let's go get Tony."

Bobo and Mark had travelled no more than five hundred yards before finding the next bureau. They seemed to be everywhere. Bobo led Mark in. The same routine. Mark stood back and kept watch and Bobo did his stuff. This time four grand and no problems. By the time they had reached the building site Tony was working on, Bobo had changed the entire fifty K. He had over thirty grand in his bag and it was twice as bulky as the fifty jackets he had started with.

They went to the gate of the building site. Mark spotted Tony right away beside a cement lorry. It was pouring tons of concrete into the wooden form work. Tony and three other joiners were on standby in case the casings moved or burst.

Bobo yelled for his brother's attention from the gate. Tony waved to them. Bobo and Mark waited while their brother had a few words with the foreman. Tony dumped his tool belt in one of the huts and grabbed his jacket before meeting them at the gate. Bobo and Tony were like twins, though Bobo was three years older and Tony four inches taller.

"Well, Bobo, aul hand. What about ye?"

"All right, kid. I'm over for a few days on a wee bit of business."

Mark snorted. "Wee bit of business? Jesus, he has millions of dollars over here with him." Mark tapped the side of his head with his forefinger. "Our big brother's gone nuts altogether this time."

Tony looked at Bobo with a look that a mother would give a naughty child. "It's the aul Stickie's gear isn't it? They're back at the aul fake dollars. Are you crazy Bobo? Big Stan got caught with that stuff over here about six years ago and he's still behind bars."

"This is different. The stuff's perfect. They can't tell it from the real deal. And I've only half a million with me not millions."

"Well I want fuck all to do with it. I've nearly eight hundred quid wages coming to me this week and that's more than enough to keep me going." "All right. So you don't want to stay in a nice hotel tonight with me and him."

"Ah well, hold on. I didn't say I wouldn't help you to spend some of it. How's Danny Dee keeping? I'm sure he has something to do with this. And he owes me a couple of good nights."

The trio headed back to Wood Green and Tony took a shower and changed. Bobo stashed the sterling he'd lifted and took out another fifty jackets. He put them into a bag with a few bits and pieces for his overnight stay. The three brothers were soon back on the underground and heading towards the West End. They got off at Green Park and walked through Mayfair and made their way to the Hilton on Park Lane.

"Holy fuck, Bobo," Tony said. "We're not staying here, are we?"

"We are. And could you stop using that word?"

"We worked in this hotel renovating it a few years ago. It's about four hundred quid a night."

"Actually, it's six hundred and forty dollars a night."

Bobo told the boys to wait outside while he checked in under the false name on his passport. He told the receptionist that he had just returned from America and was stopping over in London on his way back to Ireland. When asked for a credit card he explained he'd been mugged in New York and had his cards all stolen. So he just decided there and then to go home. He withdrew all his savings from the bank and got the first plane home, he explained.

"I hate America now," Bobo said. "I'm never going back."

"I don't blame you, sir."

"I'll be needing a family room. I'm going to have a night out with a friend or two and they might want to stay over."

"Not a problem, sir. The suite will be five hundred pounds but if your guests require breakfast it'll cost a little extra."

"No worries, love."

"Also, in light of your misfortune, and lack of a credit card, I'll need to ask you for an advance payment..."

Bobo peeled seven hundred dollars off a jacket. "I want a good rate for this. Just let me know in the morning if I owe any more."

The receptionist took the money and gave Bobo the key. She then went into the office behind the reception and checked the notes and was relieved to see they passed all the in house checks. Bobo went up to his room had a quick look around and headed back down to the foyer and on outside to where the two boys were waiting.

"Right c'mon. Let's live a little, lads."

That night, Champagne flowed, the best food available was eaten and they all washed their feet in the biggest marble bath you ever seen. Mark suggested they take a wander out the back of the hotel to look at the hookers in Mayfair. Maybe invite one or two in. After a quick inspection it was decided they were scabby cunts, and the boys went back to washing their feet and eating and drinking the best.

Tony woke first. The room was a complete mess. Valuable furniture was strewn across the floors. Food and drink spilled every where. The reek of smelly socks put the icing on the cake.

Tony went into the bathroom. He'd forgotten what it was like and stalled for a minute as he entered. Then he climbed into the shower. It was fantastic. The right temperature, the right pressure and all the soaps, creams, oils and shampoos you could ever need. He stayed in it for almost an hour.

Eventually, he got dried off and went in to raise the other two. He looked over at Bobo, laid across the king size bed he'd claimed as his own the night before. Mark had the other double and was lost under the duvet somewhere.

Tony shouted and banged anything he could get his hands on to rouse the lazy gits.

"C'mon. Get up. Get up. I'm going to work. You two can do what ye want. Change dodgy money or whatever, but I've work to go to."

Bobo stretched across to the bedside phone. "Breakfast to room... what is it?"

Mark flipped back his duvet. "223." His voice croaked. "Get extra orange juice."

"223. Full English. Yes, everything. *Yes, everything* , Yes, extra orange juice, please. Thank you."

"Maybe I'll stick around for a bit, then," Tony said. "Just for a wee sip of orange juice, like."

The breakfast was brought to the room in less than ten minutes. Tony went to the door and took the trolley from the porter. It was a delight -- all china and silverware, flowers and fruit, coffee and cream, grilled this and that. In ten seconds it looked like an explosion in a delicatessen. Bobo and Mark went back to sleep for another half hour after Tony left. They eventually got up and went down to reception. Mark stayed in the background while Bobo settled the bill at the desk. He paid in dollars and changed another two thousand while he was at it. Left a fifty quid tip.

The two brothers made their way back to the Wood Green flat and Bobo planked the money he had changed in with the rest. They made a cup of tea and Bobo started to get the picture of the set up in London. Mark explained that around ten to twelve of the West Belfast men were working in London.

"Most of them live in this one big six bedroom Georgian house on the Seven Sisters Road. Nearly all of them work on the building sites," said Mark.

They had got to know a lot of the local people including the sharp guys, the guys who knew people who knew people. These guys also got to know, through a bit of loose talk on the part of some of the Sticks, that they themselves were every bit as sharp as the London boys and a hell of a lot more formidable. Bobo decided they would go over to the Holloway Road where the Sticks usually drank and socialised.

Tony got home from work at six thirty. Mark rustled up a pot of stew and the three ate it out of big cracked bowls and washed it down with cans of beer. They got dressed in their best clothes, which mostly consisted of jeans, casual jackets and short sleeve shirts. Tony shaved and showered. The other two didn't bother. They got over to the Holloway Arms at ten o'clock. The place was in full swing with Irish ballads and rebel songs pounding and gallons of Guinness filling eager bellies.

Bobo followed Mark and Tony in through the crowded bar. When they got up to the front of the bar, Big Mackers was standing with five or six others, all from West Belfast. At first they seen Tony and Mark and a standard nod of a greeting was offered as they were over on the Holloway Road most week-ends, but when Bobo was spotted a mighty roar went up. It was always a time for celebration when new blood made its way across the Irish Sea.

One hell of a night ensued. Gary had told Bobo he could blow a few hundred quid with the boys to keep them sweet. Bobo was lifted shoulder high when he announced he was buying. The only one who was a little cautious of the situation was Big Mackers as he was the self appointed top cat of the crowd and he didn't like anyone to rock the boat. The night went on until three in the morning. They moved from the Holloway Arms to the Boston Club where the doorman let them in without paying the cover charge on the understanding that if trouble broke out, the Sticks would stand by the doormen.

Tony, Mark and Bobo woke up in the morning with spinning heads. The boys from the house never worked weekends and were delighted that Tony had over slept and missed his day's work. As the morning turned to early afternoon, breakfast started to come together.

One thing about the big house, it was run like a military billet and everyone had their own job to do. Sometimes cook, sometimes clean and sometimes do the laundry and the shopping. There was nine in total living in it and few of them were actually referred to by there proper name, it was usually something like, Wee Chomper, The Pig, The Wolf, Smicker, Big Mackers, The Greek... All of them had been shot or jailed at some time in their lives, and each of them was feared by the Provisional IRA, because of the feuds they had with each other, the Provos usually coming off worse.

The house set up wasn't always perfect and rows broke out from time to time but generally speaking it was well run and there was always something to eat.

After breakfast Bobo singled out five of the most reliable and most experienced of the boys and told them to come with him round to a wee café beside The Archway Tavern. The five sat down at a table and ordered tea. Some of the boys suggested that they should go over to the pub for a pint and were amazed that Bobo said no. He got down to business right away and explained the operation and asked if they were in. He also reminded them if they opened their mouths about it, they knew what would happen. They all wanted in.

Wee Chomper was one of the boys that Bobo had picked, he was called Wee Chomper because of the chocolate bar he favoured and always seemed to have in his pocket at school. The same bar that he would never share, not even with his mate Bobo. But Bobo always gave him the benefit of the doubt and later on in life always took him under his wing. It was Chomper who had got to know the people in the bar in Walthamstow also known as the 'Gangsters'.

Bobo split four of the boys into pairs and told them he would meet them at the house the next day with paperwork for them to start changing around London. They already knew where to get fake passports and Bobo gave them eight hundred quid to buy them. Then he and Chomper made their way over to the Gangsters Bar in Walthamstow.

When they got to the Gangsters there was very few in the place. Just a few old boys playing dominoes and passing the time over well flattened pints of bitter. The barman knew Chomper. Bobo was introduced as his mate from back home.

They sat at the bar for a while sipping lemonade and waiting for someone of interest to come in, but after half an hour Chomper asked the barman to make a few calls and see if he could rouse a few of the 'wise guys'. The barman phoned. About ten minutes later two guys came in and went over to their table.

"Okay," one of them said. "What's up? Are you having bother?"

"No, no nothing like that." Chomper said. He introduced Bobo.

Bobo gave them his friendliest smile, just to kick things off. "How's it going there, big lads?"

Stony faces.

Bobo went on. "See, what it is, I'm over here to do a wee bit of business with anybody who is interested. It's the sort of thing where you get to travel and meet people but you don't get a uniform, unless you get caught."

The London boys smirked a little. Bobo thanked God for the cool dry wit he'd been blessed with. He lifted out a jacket of dollars and threw it onto the table.

"Have you ever seen these?"

One of the London boys sneered. "Fuck's sake. We've all seen moody notes before. You had me convinced this would be something big, mate."

"No, hold on," Bobo said. "Look closer. These are different."

Bobo pulled off two of the notes and gave them to the mouthy London boy.

"Right, one of you is bound to have eighty quid on you. Go down to the bank in Main Street and buy a hundred dollar bill. Find a shop that sells magnifying glasses and buy one, then come back up here."

The quieter London guy, who seemed to be subordinate to the other, went on the errand while Bobo explained the deal.

"Sixty five cents to the dollar, any amount you need, delivered direct to you. We'll even extend a bit of credit as long as you've a surety. If you want to do it right you could open bank accounts and lodge the dollars. Every withdrawal's a laundry.

The quiet guy came back with the genuine note from the bank and the looking glass. After a bit of checking the mouthy one nodded.

"Okay, we'll deal," he said. "But we want to run all of London with this stuff."

Bobo agreed but explained that there were a few Stickies out with a small bundle but after they were done the ballpark was the Londoner's.

The four Sticks turned around thirty grand between them and brought the money to Bobo.

"All right, lads. Well done. Doc told me I can give you a few grand between you."

He started to peel off some of the sterling notes they had brought him. One of the boys put his hand up.

"Listen, Bo, we lost two days wages, so a couple of hundred each is plenty. But make sure McStravick and Doc know that we're all still behind the movement whether we're in London or wherever."

Bobo stayed another day in London and told Chomper that he could get half a mil over to London within the next three days and to tell the Londoners to have their money ready.

Bobo took Mark and Tony out for a meal at the local Greek restaurant, it was just up he road from the flat. They emptied a few bottles of wine and finished off with liquors and whiskies. Bobo reckoned they deserved it and they all went home with bellies full and heads swimming.

Tony was up at seven am as usual and off to work, he nudged Bobo on his way out and told him he would see him again next time. Bobo grunted. A few hours later Mark stirred and woke Bobo. They had breakfast and Bobo got ready for his return journey. He bantered a bit with Mark about not going to work that morning and then backed down after it was pointed out once more that he had been unemployed for the last eighteen years.

Chapter 7

Bobo got back to the small port of Stranraer in Scotland at around seven that night and boarded the 7:50 sailing. He was back in Belfast for ten o'clock. He almost forgot at one stage that he was carrying bags full of money, and that he could be stopped at any time and rumbled. It had become mundane routine. Nobody stopped him. He left the docks and drove straight to the Workers Club.

Bobo went to the bar and waited to be noticed. Gary sat on a bar stool oblivious of Bobo until Danny spotted him.

"Bobo, what about you?" Danny's voice boomed.

Gary spun round on the stool and almost fell off it.

"Well how did you do?" Gary asked. "Everything go all right? Where's the dough?"

"Take it easy. Take it easy. Suffering duck, give me a chance to sit down."

"Give him a pint, Danny Dee." Gary moved over to the stool beside Bobo and put his own pint of Harp beside Bobo's newly poured Guinness.

"Well?" Gary looked right into Bobo's face.

Bobo lifted his pint and drew deeply on it. Then he sat back on the stool and relished the attention he'd generated. He noticed Danny smirking as if to say, "Get on with it."

Bobo reached into his coat pockets and pulled out a fistful of crumpled receipts and dropped them on the bar.

"Right, here's my expenses."

Gary looked at them with bulging eyes.

Danny snickered. "What the fuck are you playing at, Bobo?"

"You think this is some sort of junket?" Gary asked. "There's no expenses."

Bobo bristled. "Well it just so happens I know what a junket is, so you're throwing big words at the wrong man here, Doc. See it's only a junket when you spend money on a trip that's non-profitable. Whereas *I* have two big bags stuffed full of Do Re Me out there in my car."

Bobo held up the keys of the car and nodded towards the bar. "So, Doc. What about a wee large brandy."

Gary nodded to Danny. "Give that man a large brandy." He grabbed the keys out of Bobo's hand.

Danny got up the morning after Bobo's return and went for his usual eight mile jog. He grabbed a bit of breakfast and made his way down to the Workers and met up with Gary. It was nine in the morning so they had a few hours in the club on their own.

They'd agreed the night before to talk about Danny's idea of sending couples out to Romania and Bulgaria on bogus holidays as another way to get the money into Ireland. Gary produced a list of couples that he thought would be the most reliable.

"Have a wee look at this," Gary said. He handed Danny a piece of paper. Danny read through the list of fifteen couples.

"Right, Pete and Clare are out," Danny said. "She's a rocket with drink in her. Barry and his missus are out. He's too nervous. And Davey and Sue would be all right but Davey is too well known. We've enough here without him, though."

They decided to go to Bulgaria first. Danny picked five couples from Gary's list to approach. Four to do the run and a fifth to fall back on. Danny phoned Bobo and told him to come down to the club while Gary went round to the houses and places of work of the four chosen couples and explained the set up to them.

The next step was to call to the travel agent on the Falls Road and grab some brochures.

Gary looked in on Danny at the club. As usual, his son-in-law was hard at it; cleaning like a spit-shine demon. And there was Bobo, on his usual stool with a highball glass in front of him. Gary clapped the little rogue on his back.

"Ach, Bobo. It's half eleven in the morning. You on the hard stuff already?"

"Sufferin' duck. Give my sore head peace will you? It's lemonade."

Gary glanced at Danny and gave him a facial shrug. Danny smiled and nodded.

"Lemonade lemonade with nothing in it?" Gary said. He prodded Bobo's ribs. "What's up, kid? Are you sick or what?"

"Nah. I'm just taking it easy today."

Danny picked up a clean pint glass and held it to the light for inspection. Satisfied, he tilted it towards Gary.

"No thanks, son," Gary said. "I'll take it easy myself."

Danny shelved the glass and filled the kettle.

"Wait till I tell you something here, Doc." Danny flicked on the kettle and looked to Bobo. "This wee man is a genius."

Bobo sat up straighter on his stool. He grinned and the lines around his mouth multiplied.

Danny went on. "Sean was on the phone a wee while ago. He needs two mil to go to Birmingham and he's on his way up with paperwork. Bobo was listening in and told me there was no problem getting stuff to Birmingham."

Gary looked at Bobo. "Well?"

"Our Jim," Bobo said.

"Your Jim what?"

"Our Jim's fish factory."

"Your Jim's fish factory what?"

Gary breathed deep and quelled the urge to shake the shit out of Bobo. He turned to Danny.

"Bobo's brother, Jim, has a fish factory just outside Newry. He sends fish to Birmingham Fish Market twice a week. Bobo made a call. There's a load going out this afternoon and Jim's willing to play ball. That's why Bobo's staying off the drink. Jim won't talk to him if he's steaming."

Bobo rolled his eyes and nodded.

Danny threw the cloth he was cleaning the bar with to Gary. "You're it, Doc. I'm away to meet Sean."

The younger men fled. The door swung shut and muffled the cranky rumble of Danny's Ford Mondeo. Gary sighed. Looked like he'd be picking up another shift.

Danny pulled into the car park of the Sheepwalk Inn just north of Newry. Bobo pointed out Reggie's car. Sean was in the passenger seat. Danny locked his car and the duo jumped into Reggie's backseat. Bobo gave Reggie directions over the back roads that took them to the fish factory in Mayobridge. Jim was looking out of the office window when they arrived.

Danny hadn't seen Bobo's older brother in a while. Jim had done a bit of operating for the Stickies in the early eighties but had retired earlier than most. He came outside to meet them and led them round to the loading bay of the small factory. The factory workers had clocked off for the day and Jim was waiting for the arrival of the lorry to pick up the two pallets of fish. One was wrapped in cling film. The other was stacked and loaded but still unsealed. Two large salmon boxes were on the ground just inside the loading bay. Empty, just as Bobo had asked.

Jim shook hands with Sean and Danny and greeted Bobo with a nod as most West Belfast brothers do.

"Must be serious if this one's sober, eh?"

Bobo shrugged.

"Well, Jim," Danny said. "Big business man now. What happened to Socialist values?"

"Well it's like this, Danny. When you have to listen to twenty fish filleters crying about wages and conditions every day it feels like socialism is kicking the shit out of you. But I'll let you know how this capitalism craic pans out."

Sean smiled at Jim. "Ah, it's hard to be a socialist in a capitalist society, Jim. So there'll be a few quid in this for you down the line, if you can do us a wee favour or two."

"Nah, you're all right, Sean. I don't know what you're doing and I don't want to know. I'm going back into the office here to wait on the lorry.

There's a big roll of cling film beside the pallets. You can give me a shout when you're finished."

Jim disappeared. Danny and Bobo got to work. They pulled two large sports bags from the boot of Reggie's car and loaded the paperwork into the salmon boxes. One mil fitted nicely into each box with four inches to spare on top. They sealed up the dollars with plastic bags and threw a few shovels of ice on top. Then they used the strap machine to secure the lids on the big polystyrene boxes and lifted them on to the top of the pallet beside four similar boxes.

Danny used a blue felt tip pen to put a small tick on the two boxes containing the paperwork. "I don't think Anton would be too pleased if he found he'd just paid seven hundred and fifty thousand quid for twenty big fish." Bobo wiped sweat from his furrowed brow. "Aye, and some wee fish monger in Birmingham would be packing his bags and heading for South America."

They got Jim to phone the transport company. He asked if one of his employees could travel over in the lorry with the driver as he had to collect cheques from his customers in the market. It wasn't an unusual request.

Bobo wished he'd kept his mouth shut about Jim's fish factory. Sean had been in touch with Anton and told him to meet Bobo in the Birmingham Fish Market in Pershore Street at half three the next day. It dawned on him that he had around twenty hours of solid travelling in an articulated lorry ahead of him. And he'd have to sit with his brother and wait until the poxy thing arrived.

Sean and Danny said their goodbyes to Jim and thanked him. They invited him up to the Workers club for a drink some time which Jim accepted, but both sides knew it was never going to happen. Bobo watched Sean, Danny and Reggie leave the factory car park from Jim's office. He sat in the visitor's chair and Jim paced the floor. They hadn't much to say to each other.

"How's everybody in Belfast?" Jim asked. "Patricia, Madeline and all the rest of them?"

"Aye, dead on, dead on" Bobo said.

Jim frowned. "Bobo, are you ever going to get sense?"

"For Fu--"

The lorry pulled in to the factory car park. Engine roars and hydraulic hisses broke up the potential brotherly argument.

Jim used the fork lift to set the two pallets into the refrigerated trailer. Bobo grabbed a white coat off a hook in the office. He went out and climbed up into the cab of the big eight-wheeler.

Bobo looked at Jim through the rolled up window and nodded. Jim nodded back.

He turned to the driver. "Well, mucker. I don't suppose you have anything to drink?"

The driver smiled. "Howay, man. Are you joking?" His Geordie accent was thicker than Jimmy Nail's. "Of course I have."

He opened the door of a small fridge at the back of the cab to reveal about a dozen cans of beer. Bobo joined his hands and looked heavenward.

The English driver had never had such an easy run in his life as Bobo kept him spellbound with corny jokes, wild stories and a whole mish-mash of bullshit. The driver even broke his own unwritten rule and had a can of beer with Bobo.

They got to the Fish Market at around three am, the driver got out and arranged for the two pallets of fish to be lifted off at Carfellas Fish Merchants and Bobo said he would stay with it until the manager arrived and sort out the cheques he had to collect. The driver shook hands with Bobo and told him to look out for the Mourne Fruit and

Veg lorry at around four o'clock over at the mushroom stalls across the market.

"The driver knows you're getting a lift back to Belfast with him."

"Sound as a pound, mucker." Bobo said as he grabbed his hand. "I'll see you

again. And don't forget the one about the 'blow job hedge hog'. Your mates will love that one."

The driver climbed up into his cab still laughing and drove off to finish his deliveries Between Birmingham and London.

So this is Birmingham?

Maybe it was the beer buzz, but Bobo couldn't muster much excitement for his new surroundings. Three in the morning looks pretty much the same in most places he'd been to. Cold and miserable. The lorry he'd hitched a lift in pulled away. As the tail lights faded away Anton showed up in a big four-by-four jeep. Bobo spotted him in the front passenger seat and he gave him a quick wave. The driver got out and came over to Bobo and they started to pull the layers of cling wrap from the top of the pallets load.

The big Russian could have been Anton's brother they looked so alike. Even their dress sense was the same – all leather and denim. The driver helped Bobo to carry the two boxes of paperwork to the back of the jeep. They threw the boxes into the back and Bobo went round to the passenger window of the jeep to talk to Anton. He rapped on the window and Anton rolled it down.

"Ah, it is the funny man. Bobo, how are you doing, my friend?"

"Dead on, KGB. Dead on."

"Please, Bobo. My name is Anton."

"Oh right. Sorry about that, big fellah. How're you keeping, Anton?"

Anton smiled as he pulled a sports bag from the foot well and handed it to Bobo. The driver had got back into the car and sat waiting for instructions. Bobo nodded to him then nodded at the three passengers in the shadowed backseat. He realised the middle passenger had a large hessian sack over his head. It came down to his waist. A rope tied around him at chest level pinned his arms and secured the sack.

Bobo looked at him and then at Anton. "Who's your man?"

Anton dealt Bobo a thousand yard stare. "He is my friend. A good friend"

"Why's he wearing the big long hat, then?"

"He betrayed my trust."

Anton looked over his shoulder and muttered something in Russian to the sack. Bobo watched the hessian cloth shake. The guy underneath sputtered what seemed to be words of denial amid heavy sobs. A glint of reflecting light caught Bobo's eye. Anton thrust a bowie knife through the gap in the front seats and deep into the sack. Anton twisted the knife. The body twitched and convulsed. The leather and denim boys on each side of the bagged man pressed down on his shoulders to still him.

Anton withdrew the knife and looked at Bobo for a reaction. Bobo looked at the still twitching man and the growing dark brown stain on the sack and then turned to Anton.

With a sharp intake of breath he said, "Oh that must have hurt."

Bobo lifted the sports bag level with the window, and smiling said. "Thanks for the dough, mucker. See you again soon."

The jeep sped off and Bobo calmly walked towards the small market café. When Anton and his crew were out of sight he stopped and emptied his stomach. Bobo was no stranger to killing. He'd witnessed it many times during the Belfast Troubles. But it was usually in a gun battle or an explosion. Knife work was too much like the real thing to him. *Murder*. He sat in the cafe by the window and watched for the Mourne Fruit and Veg lorry to pull up at the mushroom stalls. It arrived at four on the button.

Bobo left the cafe and went over to it.

"All right there, mate? Are you giving me a wee lift across the water, like?"

The driver looked at Bobo and loosed a heavy sigh.

"Aye. My boss rung me and told me. You can climb up there into the cab. But listen, no smoking."

"All right. Tell you what. I'll wait a wee while until you're ready to go."

Bobo took a stroll around the market, there were three sections, fish, poultry and fruit and vegetables. The market was beginning to come alive now, forklift trucks moving around like giant ants unloading lorries and setting down pallets at various loading bays. Bobo got the feeling that he wasn't the only one in the big market who was there on dubious business. All those crates of fruit and vegetables coming in from around the world were bound to have a pound or two of cocaine amongst them. A lot of the forklift drivers looked more like cops than cops do. If Danny Dee was here he would be able to pick them out right away.

The seven hundred k in his bag weighed heavy and it started to worry him. He made his way back to his lift and was glad to see the last pallet unloaded.

"Okay then, mate," Bobo said.

The lorry driver nodded and Bobo climbed aboard. He didn't have the same rapport with this driver as he had with the last one, so he asked him if it was all right to get into the bunk at the back of the cab for a kip. Bobo slept until the lorry pulled into Stranraer, the Scottish port. The driver shouted into Bobo. "Do you want to come up on deck or do you want to sleep on?"

Bobo was happy to stay in the warm and comfortable bunk. He waved the driver away and slept on through the short sea journey. The ferry docked in Larne Port and Bobo was awakened by the hubbub of ferry passengers returning to their cars, vans, buses and lorries. The driver climbed up into the cab and started the engine. Bobo stayed in the bunk until the lorry had driven off the boat and left the docks compound. He stretched, scratched all his itches and crawled through the curtain into the passenger seat.

"All right there, mate?"

"You're a very noisy sleeper," the driver said.

"Really? I never heard a thing."

The driver rolled his eyes and grimaced. They arrived in Belfast forty five minutes later and Bobo asked the driver to drop him off at the bottom of the Grosvenor Road. The short walk had him in The Workers club in four minutes.

It was a little after two in the afternoon, less than twenty-two hours since he'd left the club for the fish factory. It was like a surreal dream. He had delivered two million dodgy dollars to an ex-Russian spy, watched a man bleed to death in front of his eyes, and now he was standing back in his favourite watering hole with a big bag full of cash. He went over to the bar where Danny and Gary stood. They sniggered at the sight of the dishevelled Bobo.

Bobo threw the bag of cash at Gary and demanded a pint from Danny. Gary took the bag and disappeared it into the back office. Then he came back out to the bar. He smiled at Bobo.

"Good man, Bo. Good man."

Bobo had half emptied his pint in one gulp. He wiped his mouth. "Oh, before I forget, Anton sent a wee message over to everybody."

"Right. What did he say?" Gary asked.

"He said nothing. Sufferin' duck, he just stabbed some poor bastard to death in front of my eyes, right in the middle of the market."

Danny's eyes widened as he listened to Bobo. Gary didn't seem too taken aback. Bobo was a little disappointed at Gary's lack of reaction and looked to him for an explanation.

"Well I'm not really that surprised. Sean told me a story about Anton a while ago. You see, Sean started dealing with the Eastern Europeans around eighty-six or eighty-seven. Anton was still in the KGB. They did a bit of business in Poland together. Sean told me they were driving through Warsaw to a meeting with a few of the Koreans when Anton swung off the main road and into the side streets.

They were in a real rough looking area and Anton pulled up at an old rundown building. Sean could see two fellahs standing in the doorway. They were both blindfolded and bound and there were a few other blokes standing around. The other blokes seemed to be expecting Anton. Well, he pulled up, got out of the car and walked over to the two blindfolded guys. He whacked both of them between the eyes. Anton just got back in the car and mumbled "fucking criminals," and that was it, he just drove off to the meeting."

There was a long silence then Danny chirped up.

"Well, we've been looking at holidays."

Chapter 8

Danny was proud of his plan. He and Gary had looked at a tonne of stuff from the travel agents and decided on Sunny Beach on the southern end of the Bulgarian Black Sea coast. The flight would take them into Bourgas. Anton had told Sean that since the collapse of the Soviet Bloc, most of the security measures in the airports in ex-satellite states were slack or non-existent, especially in the tourist areas.

Danny had booked four couples through different travel agents around Belfast and into separate hotels in the resort. Bobo and Danny were booked along with two female members of the movement. Bobo was going to take a case of paperwork back but Sean had told Danny their job was just to organise things and come home empty. He'd explained to Danny that a contact in the Irish Special Branch had warned him that there were enquiries coming in from the American Secret Service and both he and Danny's names had been mentioned.

When Danny had come to choose the two girls that were to travel with him and Bobo, he made a point of picking two of the more plain girls in the movement, just in case Bronagh ever got to hear about it. This didn't dampen Bobo's enthusiasm in any way.

"Well you never look at the clock when you're poking the fire."

The end of September was drawing the tourist season to an end and the resort, although still busy enough to let the entourage blend in, wasn't just as crazy as at peak times. They all made their own way from Belfast to Dublin Airport with families and friends who believed they were just going on a nice holiday. Even though the four couples were acquainted they made no contact with each other or with Danny and Bobo, who also stayed apart.

Danny found it hard to make conversation with his travelling companion while Bobo and his girl were hitting it off like wildfire. And hitting the bar as well. An hour before boarding, Danny followed Bobo into the airport toilets and told him to cool it. The little man held back enough to make it onto the plane without incident.

They arrived in Bulgaria and after collecting their luggage, which consisted of two half empty suitcases per couple, they met their travel company rep who directed them to their transfer coaches. The rest of the holidaymakers on board the coach were from England and Scotland and a few from Dublin. The dollar mules sat quietly along with the rest, even though the holiday mood was on them and they were all just bursting to break in to a charge of Rebel songs and Irish reels and jigs. The session would have to wait until they all got back to the Workers Club with the mission accomplished.

The four couples were each dropped off at their hotels. Danny, Bobo and their two travelling companions were last to be dropped off. Along the way, Danny had made a mental note of where each hotel was located. The two couples handed in their passports at reception and received the keys to their rooms. Danny wasn't too worried about who was going to see them talking together. They could be any Irish group of holidaymakers who had met by chance on holiday. Their rooms were on the same floor but five or six doors apart which suited the situation nicely. In Danny's mind, the two girls would be sharing a room and Bobo would bunk with him.

Danny, being careful, told the girls to scatter some of their clothes in both the rooms for the sake of the room service maids' information. Bobo confessed that he wasn't too happy with the setup. He kind of hoped that for security reasons they would have to cohabitate with their respective partners. Danny didn't change his mind.

The two girls soon got into the swing of things and were happy to spend most of their time lying by the pool, drinking beer, eating ice cream and getting fatter. Bobo spent a good bit of his time in the hotel bar. He couldn't believe how cheap the drink was and he wasn't long getting to grips with the Bulgarian Lev to Sterling exchange rate.

Danny got to work almost immediately. He had gone down through the strip which connected most of the hotels in the resort, contacted the four couples and got keys for their rooms off them. They all had two keys each, Danny told them he would be going into their rooms and repacking one of their cases and he would prefer if they did not look into them after he had done it. For their sake it would be better that way. They were happy knowing they could sun themselves all week, drink the nice little bundle of spending money that had been allocated to them and still help the movement out.

After collecting the keys Danny went down to the Avis car rental booth which was also on the strip. He hired a Lada Riva estate car and drove down towards Bourgas to the ancient town of Nessabar. Although starting to develop, the town was not as busy as the other resorts on the Bulgarian coasts. Danny drove to the prearranged meeting point just south of the harbour where he met one of Yang's agents. The agent knew Danny immediately from the description he was given, and approached him with cool confidence.

The reason he was so relaxed was that he knew he was never in any real danger of arrest or imprisonment. He had been intercepted on quite a few occasions while carrying paperwork but always claimed diplomatic immunity and after he had the Dollars taken from him he would be sent back to the embassy in whichever country he was in and then later on, his embassy would send him somewhere else.

He smiled. "You are Danny, yes.?"

"That's me." Danny returned the smile.

"I am Hang Tu-yuk." The Asian man hopped out of his car, another Lada, and Danny joined him. They took a seat on a stone bench on the harbour wall and lapped up the Bulgarian afternoon sun. They looked around for a while before Hang spoke.

"I have made it easy for you, Danny. I have taken the paperwork, as you like to call it, from their packing cases and put it into small suitcases like the suitcases used by tourist here in Bulgaria." He got up and walked to his car and pointed into the back seat. There was three middle-sized suitcases there covered with a blanket. Two more in the boot. Each contained one point five mil, which was fine as that amount of paperwork could be packed into a larger suit case scattered among clothes books and other bric-a-brac.

Another Agent sat in the front passenger seat and Danny could see the bulge under his shirt. He knew it was a small machine pistol, a Glock M17 or a wee Scorpion. They both lifted a case from the boot of Hang's car and threw them into Danny's. They went back and took the other three and put them into Danny's car and threw the blanket over them.

Hang was out of breath as he spoke to Danny. "One last thing, comrade."

Hang went to the passenger window and the other agent handed him a bulky brown envelope. He brought it to Danny.

"This is for you. Dispose of it when you feel you no longer need it."

Danny knew right off by the bulk and the weight that it was a small pistol. Hang smiled and bowed to Danny then got into his car and drove off.

Danny sat in the driver seat of his Lada and took the new TT33 automatic pistol out of the envelope along with a spare magazine. He pulled back the slide and let go pushing a round up into the breach and sat the gun at the right side of his seat. He made sure the gun was well settled between the seat and the centre console. He hadn't forgotten what Yang had told him about there being no safety catch on the gun.

After putting the spare clip into his pocket Danny slipped the Lada into gear and started off back to Sunny Beach. He was back in the resort in less than half an hour. First things first. He went to his own hotel, lifted one of the suitcases from the car and locked it. Then went into the lobby, spotted Bobo at the bar and nodded over. Bobo hopped off his barstool and met Danny at the lift. No one paid any attention to Danny coming in with the suit case. It was a regular sight in the hotel.

Danny and Bobo got into the lift. It was obvious Bobo had a few in him, but he wasn't too bad. They took the suitcase of paperwork into the girls' room and lifted one of the girl's bigger cases on to the bed. They started to lift bits of clothing and shoes from around the room, 'the girls weren't to house proud', and started to pack the case. First a layer of socks, skirts and underwear then a scattering of ten grand jackets. A few books and magazines and other normal luggage then another layer of paperwork.

"Stop messing Bobo" Danny said as he grabbed the pair of knickers Bobo was holding up to his nose.

Bobo laughed. " Hey, I was enjoying that."

It wasn't long until they had the contents of the small case inside the larger one along with the girls stuff.

Danny had planned to take Bobo with him to go to the other hotels and repeat the job. He looked over at Bobo who had flopped out on one of the twin beds and started to drift off to sleep. Looked like he was finishing the job on his own.

Danny went round the other four hotels and had no problems. A few times on his way into the rooms he met up with room service maids who just smiled and nodded. He had also taken small luggage locks with him that he used to lock the suitcases he had packed and put them into the wardrobes of the couples' rooms. He kept the keys himself. The job done, he eventually got back to his own hotel and had a well earned drink at the bar. Bobo appeared after an hour or so and came over to him speaking in a formal manner as though they had just got acquainted.

They spent the next five days in the same manner and in the evenings they would go to their rooms separately and no one ever knew that the two couples had split up. One of the evenings Bobo with a little too much to drink accidentally on purpose wandered into the girls' room but was told to get to hell out by the girl who was supposed to be Danny's partner.

The night before they were supposed to leave Danny went round to the back street behind the strip where he had seen large grills over what was a fairly dated sewer and drainage system and with great reluctance he dropped the already dismantled TT33 into it. Then he went back to the hotel and met the girls in the lounge.

Danny told the girls that Bobo would go down to their room in the morning and his girl could meet him down in the hotel reception. They were to go home the way they came, as two couples who didn't really know each other.

Danny had almost finished packing. One case was closed and the other was almost full. There was a knock at the door of the room and Danny went to answer it expecting the cleaners to want in to get their job done. He opened the door and was confronted by two uniformed Bulgarian police men. They forced him to the other side of the room. Danny protested as he was spread-eagled face first against the wall. They roughly searched him. One of the cops asked him his name. Danny gave the name on his fake passport which was sitting on the dressing table. One of the cops lifted the passport and studied the photo. He looked closely at Danny and left the hotel room.

The door was still ajar and Danny could hear the cop speaking to someone outside in the hallway. He could hear replies in a hushed voice and was sure he could pick out an American accent, much softer than the guttural Bulgarian speech of the policeman. The policeman came back into the room and asked Danny his date of birth. Danny gave the info on the passport which he had memorised. The policeman went to the suitcases on the bed. He rummaged through the open one then opened the other and searched it too. He then went back outside and reported to the unseen men.

The cop came back into the room and went up to Danny, still pressed against the wall. The Bulgarian warmed the back of Danny's ear as he spoke in broken English.

"You no move from here."

Danny heard someone enter. He guessed it was the American. Judging by the carpet-muffled sound of footsteps, the new guy stopped in the middle of the room. Seconds later he started to systematically pull drawers open. Then he went to the wardrobe. Danny's left cheek was pressed against the wall. He could see the wardrobe and the American's back. When the American opened the wardrobe there was a long mirror on the inside of the door. Danny caught a glimpse of the American in it before he closed it again. He got a good look at him and knew from the cut of him that he was CIA, FBI or one of the other American Security Agencies. After a few minutes the American left. The policeman dragged Danny away from the wall and turned him so they were face to face.

"You go home today, Irish man?"

Danny nodded.

"Do not come back to Bulgaria, my friend. Next time we throw you in jail."

The police man pulled Danny's wallet from his back pocket and stepped back. Danny turned around and watched him pull all the cash from it, a mixture of Sterling and Bulgarian Lev. He put a few notes back in and threw the wallet on the bed. He stuck the rest of the cash into his shirt pocket and left.

Danny quickly repacked the cases and got down the stairs just as the transfer coach had arrived. He looked around and could see nothing unusual. He joined the queue to throw his cases into the bottom of the coach.

Danny's girl had already boarded the coach and was sitting at the window around the middle of it. Bobo sat at the back with his partner. Danny climbed up the steps of the coach and sat down beside the disgruntled girl who just looked out the window and said nothing.

The plane landed at Dublin Airport four hours after leaving Bourgas, as Danny stepped on to the tarmac he wanted to get down on his knees and kiss the ground, just like the Pope. He didn't care if he was arrested now, he could hack it in Ireland but the thought of being banged up in Bulgaria frightened him.

Everything went smoothly at Dublin Airport, Danny was surprised that he wasn't stopped at passport control and was curious and a little suspicious as to why the American Agent or the Bulgarians had not warned the Irish authorities of the reason for their little visit to his hotel room.

Danny watched as each of his crew grabbed their cases from the carousel and was relieved to see all of the cases came out safely. He lifted his own cases which he had let go past him a few times while he watched the others pick up theirs. He had already instructed them all to take a taxi to a different bar each in the town of Swords which was only a few miles from the airport.

Gary was waiting in a fourteen seat minibus across the street from the first bar. He jumped out and waved to the couple who were disappointed that they were not going to get a much needed drink, they protested but Gary assured them they would be stopping further up the road to Belfast where they would be treated to a sumptuous lunch and as much drink as their big empty bellies could hold.

Reggie was sitting in his car behind the bus and as the couple got to it Gary took their cases from them and told them to get in. He threw one case into the boot of the bus and knowing that the case with the small padlock on it was the one with the paperwork inside, he took it to Reggie's car and put it in the boot. He went to the other bars and done the same although at the other venues the couples had already got into the bar and were drinking thirstily. This time he just took the case with the dollars inside and threw it into Reggie's car. He told each of the couples to drink up and he would be back to collect them in five minutes.

The last call was the bar that Bobo was in. When Gary went in Bobo and his girl were sitting in a dark corner with two pints and two large brandies in front of them and Bobo was snogging and groping the girl who was just as enthusiastic as Bobo. Gary went over and gave Bobo a slap on the head.

"Right Casanova lets go."

Bobo looked up. "Ach what about ye Doc"?

The girl just gave an embarrassed nod.

Gary lifted the last of the paperwork cases and told Bobo to drink up and follow him outside, he brought the case out to Reggie who then drove off to Mick's house which was only a mile down the road. Bobo and his girl got onto the bus and Gary went back and picked up the other three couples.

The bus left Swords and drove for fifteen miles up the main Belfast road and stopped at the The Old Mill Hotel just outside Julianstown, they all spilled out of the bus and into the hotel bar where Danny was waiting. Danny had taken a taxi straight there and had six bottles of Champagne in ice buckets on the large table in front of him.

As they entered and spotted Danny a huge cheer went up while they all homed in on the booze. For the sake of the locals drinking in the bar, Gary suggested they sing a verse of Happy Birthday to a fictional name in Bobo's direction. Big juicy steaks and mountains of French fries were served up and the party began.

Towards the end Sean showed up and picked up the tab and congratulated everyone for a job well done. He arranged to meet Gary and Danny the next day. Gary was the only one who didn't drink as he had to drive. Even Danny got well sloshed and the whole team snored in unison all the way back to Belfast, Bobo's girl rumbling louder than the rest.

Danny woke with a pounding headache and dragged himself down stairs only to meet a very disgruntled Bronagh.

"Oh if it isn't Mr International Drunkard."

Danny just flopped down on the sofa and mumbled just how sorry he was. After a minute or two Bronagh relented and went over to him and gave him a hug and told him how much she missed him. Danny had expected nothing less. He could read his wee wife like a book.

Danny took a handful of aspirin and drank a cup of coffee and made his way down to the club. Gary had opened up and had already started to clean up and stack the shelves.

"Are you trying to put me out of a job there, Doc?"

"Nah I thought I would give you a wee hand I thought you would need it after the skin-full you had yesterday."

Danny sat down at one on one of the high stools, elbows on the bar and head held in his two hands. Gary laughed and started making as much noise as he could.

"Who's Champagne Charlie now?"

Danny just shook his head and didn't realise that Gary was winding him up with the noise he was making.

"I can't even remember walking into the house last night."

"That's because you didn't. I carried you in."

The aspirin started to kick in and Danny looked up to see Gary smiling as he slammed the same glass repeatedly down on a shelf with a loud bang.

"Oh, you evil Bastard" Danny said.

"That's for the large brandy you and Bobo squeezed out of me a few weeks back. Aul Doc never forgets."

Danny joined in with the cleaning and stacking.

Sean came through the door and into the club.

"Danny me boy, Danny. Well done, well done. You were a wee bit on the tipsy side yesterday so I didn't want to talk business. Did everything go all right, then?"

Danny had already told Gary about the run in with the Bulgarian cops and the Yank, and so filled Sean in as well.

"Well I can't say I'm surprised Danny, the shit has hit the fan. What I'm getting from our contact in the Special Branch in Dublin is that the first of the paperwork we have changed along the border has been detected over in Washington. My name and yours has been mentioned and they may also know about Anton, so it's time to get super security conscious. We can expect a lot of heat from here on in.

You know the Yanks are so worried about this operation that they've changed the design of the dollar.

"What, what do you mean changed them?" Asked Danny.

"Yep, they have redesigned them completely, they're using some new type of ink and more security features. They have even made Benjamin Franklin's head bigger on the new notes.

The way it is we need to get the rest of the paperwork changed as quickly as possible before they start calling the old notes in. Now listen to me,

Anton's crowd in Birmingham can't get enough of this stuff, so we'll leave the border alone for a while and concentrate on Birmingham and get Bobo to carry on with the London craic.

We need to get rid of the small head notes, and Yang seems confident they will be able to copy the new big heads as soon as they are released. So get Bobo cracking right away"

"Somebody mention my name?"

Bobo walked in to the club with a big smile on his face the same face that was carrying traces of makeup and lipstick. Seemed like his fat travelling partner stayed the night.

"Yes, Bobo, *I* mentioned your name" Sean said. "Good man Bobo, good man, I'm proud of ye."

Bobo shuffled up to the other three hoping for more of the same praise and recognition. He didn't get it.

"Look at the state of you," Danny said. "You haven't even washed yourself this morning, you wee minger."

"Excuse me Mister drunk and disorderly. Mister couldn't even get out of the bus. Mister Champagne Charlie who had to be carried into his house."

Gary laughed and nodded.

"Right lads that's enough," Sean said. "Back down to business, Bobo I want you to get yourself back over to London and get the Belfast men over there working full time for us. Pick out a half dozen or so of the best. Right, you can tell them to pack in their building jobs and we'll pay their wages with a good bonus for them." Bobo agreed and said he would get on it right away. Bobo's attitude surprised everyone, normally he would be looking for a drink and treating the whole thing like one big joke, but lately he had changed.

"Bobo can we do another fish run to Birmingham market? Would you approach Jim again?" Asked Sean.

"Aye, no problem, same as the last time... Better still, I've been thinking... listen to this for an idea. We can get Jim to send fish to Billingsgate Fish Market in London; he does that from time to time. The way he usually works it is, the Birmingham drop is made first, then the other two pallets go on to London. If Champagne Danny here goes over with the lorry to Birmingham he can do the same job that I done two weeks ago. Hopefully Anton won't stab anybody this time because yer big woman there might wet herself." He nodded in Danny's direction who thought that Bobo was now getting to big for his boots, however, so far Sean was impressed.

Bobo went on; "So I fly to London and make my way to Billingsgate. I know my way around the place I went over a few times for Jim. They just drop the pallets off in the middle of the car park where these wee barrow boys go and collect the stuff off the pallets and get paid by what they deliver to the different dealers. Nobody expects anyone to steal fish.

I'll get our Mark to hire a car over there for a week and he can go over to the market and grab a barrow and throw it into the back of the car. He can buy one of the big aprons they wear over there as well and then when I get over to London we can just drive to the market, go and lift the boxes with the paperwork in them, throw them into the car and away we go."

They were all impressed and Danny had begun to forget the slagging off Bobo gave him earlier. The only thing that bugged him was the fact that Bobo would be flying and he would be on the long haul in the lorry.

Bobo loved it.

The whole thing went down like clockwork. Danny did his run to Birmingham and got back to Belfast on the mushroom lorry. Anton just turned up and collected the dollars and paid for them, much to Danny's relief he didn't kill anyone this time and Danny started to feel a bit more comfortable in his company. Danny arranged to meet him in Moscow for the next deal and Anton told him he would arrange security and safe passage for him.

Meanwhile in London, Bobo had flown into Heathrow and got the Piccadilly Line straight down to Wood Green and met up with Mark. It was almost a hundred quid more expensive to fly to Heathrow than it would have been to go to Gatwick but Bobo knew that anyone flying in from Belfast to Gatwick would be treated like an animal, so he paid the extra.

Tony got home from work at around six thirty pm. When he went into the flat he was not surprised at what he saw before him. Bobo and Mark were sitting at the table which was stacked high with green backs. Tony stepped back in a dramatic gesture with his hands in the air.

"Wow"

Mark laughed at the dramatics. Tony had expected something like this at some stage as Mark had told him Bobo was coming back.

Tony said, "Never mind all this shite. Where's my dinner?"

Bobo turned round to face him, "Greek or Indian?"

Tony wasn't too happy with the goings on but he was willing to accept a bit of compensation by way of a slap up feed in the Greek's. Tony jumped into the shower while the other two packed away the paperwork. They headed off up the street to the Greek restaurant. Shish kebabs, moussaka, Greek salad and gallons of Greek wine -- yummy scrummy.

Tony went to work the next morning and Bobo and Mark went over to the Seven Sisters Road with two large sports bags full of paperwork. They went to the big house where eight of the Westies were waiting. They had all jacked in their jobs the day before. Bobo and Mark went into the main living room and started to pull the dollars out of their bags. Each of the boys took one hundred grand each and armed with a fake passport headed down to the West End.

Bobo and Mark then went over to Walthamstow to the Gangsters Bar and met up with the wise guys and sold them another eight hundred grand at sixty five cents to the dollar. The wise guys grabbed the deal eagerly as the previous money had simply been lodged into the bank and then was withdrawn a few days later through ATMs. They were willing to take all they could get and Bobo told them there would be no problem, he would be back in two weeks time with two million for them.

Chapter 9

Within five days the Westies had changed everything they had. Bobo paid them what they were due and told them to go back to work for the next two weeks but to be ready for the next batch in two weeks time. Mark extended the car hire lease for another two days and he and Bobo headed over to Holyhead for the quick ferry journey to Dublin Port. Danny had got in touch with Sean who was waiting for them just outside the port. He told Reggie to give them the headlights as they came out of the port compound and then followed Reggie's car a few miles up the road to the Silver Herring Bar just west of Dublin. The two cars were parked up and Sean went into the bar.

Sean was in great form. He had got into the bar in front of Bobo and Mark and had two large brandies and two pints sitting on the bar waiting for them. Reggie stayed in his car. As Bobo came in he looked at Sean and then at the liquid, the beautiful liquid that was Ireland, no matter where he went the beautiful liquid was not the same as it was in Ireland. Bobo and Mark went up to Sean at the bar.

"All right Sean? This is our Mark."

Sean put his hand out to Mark who was quivering in his shoes at the thought of shaking hands with the 'Great legend Sean McStravick.'

"How are you doing Mark? Good to meet you."

"Dead on, dead on, Sean. Bobo has a few quid for you in the car outside."

Bobo and Sean looked at each other and laughed. Mark told them he was going to do a turn around and grab the next ferry back to mainland Britain and get back to London later on that evening. Sean told Bobo to go out to the hire car and take the Sterling and throw it into Reggie's car. Reggie, as usual, said nothing and drove off.

When Bobo got back into the bar Mark had been busy quizzing Sean as to how much blood he had lost when he carried a dying comrade back across the border, why he didn't just leave him and save himself as the other volunteer was dying anyway, why was he now not a Provo, and what was his favourite weapon? Bobo had caught the tail end of the conversation and told Mark to shut up and leave Sean alone. Sean just laughed and waved it off.

"Right Mark it's time you headed back down to the docks and got yourself on that boat."

Mark agreed and left after drinking half the pint and none of the brandy.

"Right, Sean, what about this drink we're supposed to be having this last two years?"

"Here we go Bobo," Sean said as he lifted Marks brandy and sunk it.

"Ya ho, McStravick, ya ho."

Sean winked at Bobo.

"Do you remember the time when we hit Albert Street Barracks?" Said Bobo as he necked his Brandy and slammed the empty glass on the bar and waited as Sean called for another two.

Mick Rogers picked up the two drunken IRA men from the bar at around twelve o'clock that night and brought them back to his house to let them sleep it off. He also phoned Sean's wife to let her know what was happening. She responded by calling Bobo an Antichrist and the worst wee bastard she had ever met.

Bobo got into the Workers around four o'clock. He had come up from Dublin on the train and walked up the short distance from Great Victoria Street Station. His head was spinning. Sean McStravick had hollow legs. Bobo could just about remember Sean and Mick carrying him out of the bar and out to the car, and then throwing him onto Mick's couch.

Bobo entered the club and Danny was behind the bar.

"Bow Bells Bobo, ahwight mate? How's fings in Landin, then."

Bobo smiled at Danny, his hangover counted for nothing because he had enjoyed one good night with his old comrade Sean.

"*Landin* is going great Missus Devine. What have you been doing for the last week or so? Oh let me guess, kissing Jamsey's arse and washing glasses? Give me a pint you big fruit."

Danny laughed and eventually shook hands with Bobo.

"Here, listen to this, did Sean mention what's coming up next?"

"No, we just got drunk."

"Hah. That's why he didn't tell you. What we're going for now, is the one hundred million dollar mark. That's what he wants to hit, one hundred mil."

"Listen, I don't really care. As long as the social security don't find out, because if that cheque is not in my letter box next Tuesday I will come down here and I will be looking for compensation."

Gary came in and went to the bar, he gave Bobo a slap on the back and said, "You're some pup, Bobo, you're some pup. Jamesy is cracking up because things are going so well. He thought you and Danny Dee were going to mess up big time."

Bobo looked at Gary, "You know something, Doc? People have short memories. You yourself haven't even been around that long, so let me tell you something. This aul biz is a piece of piss to me. See me, see Danny Dee? This is all good aul craic, good aul craic. You should ask your son-in-law sometime about the Lower Falls Curfew, or the week after Big Joe McCann was shot dead!

Gary took over at the bar and Danny left, it was his night off. Bobo was on his favourite bar stool. This was the first night for a while he was back in his school of comfort. He was exchanging jokes, offering insults and just having a bit of banter with Gary when Jamesy came in, and right away the light-hearted atmosphere was cut short. He went to the bar and asked Gary how much money he had taken in and how much last night. He then turned to Bobo and looked at him with disdain.

"How come you're not drunk?" he spat at Bobo.

Bobo lifted his glass high and said, "Well if it isn't Ireland's answer to Jean Claude Van Damme."

Jamesy looked at him confused. He shook his head "What?"

Gary just smirked. The Workers was at the usual ebb for a December Tuesday afternoon. Apart from Gary, Bobo and Jamesy, there were only two other old fogeys sitting in the lounge, old Frank and his mate Brian. The club was enjoying a lull, it was quiet, it was resting before the shenanigans that exploded on Thursday night and carried on until Sunday night.

Bobo was just about to leave and go home to cook a bit of grub. He preferred the club when Jamesy was not around and he liked it more when

Danny was behind the bar. Suddenly the door was kicked in. Right away Bobo thought, cops or Brits. Five big guys stormed in. The main guy went straight to Frank, the other four panned out around the club they had all pulled out pistols which they held pointed at the ceiling. The main guy grabbed Frank by his hair and growled into his face.

"Bobo, where's Bobo?"

Old Frank looked up with defiance. "Fuck off, Brit."

"Fuck you."

The big London gangster cocked the weapon and pushed it into old Frank's head. Frank ignored it and asked Brian if he wanted another drink. Brian was ready to faint.

Bobo heard everything and could see old Frank may be on his last legs, he called out. "Hey, big shite. I'm Bobo. What do you want?"

The big Englishman walked up to Bobo and smashed his gun across the side of Bobo's head. Bobo toppled off his stool and landed on the floor then, two heavy boots were stuck into his rib cage. He groaned in agony as the pain shot through his body. Gary ran round the bar to Bobo's aid and two of the English men intercepted him leaving Bobo lying on the floor bleeding. Jamesy froze with his hands in the air. He started to spew out, "What do you want? Take the money. No problem, take the money."

Gary had his face almost pressed up against one of the Brits. He knew he couldn't take them but he announced, "I'm going over to check on my mate. Shoot me if you want."

Gary pushed the Brit out of his way and went to Bobo who now looked like he was semiconscious. For a second it looked like the situation was going to explode. The English men were taken aback and did not know how to react to Gary's indifference. Jamesy who was shitting himself shouted, "Calm down, calm down," then shouted to the main guy "What's the problem? Can we sort this out?"

"This little cunt has been working on my patch. I have been getting dollars from my mates in Birmingham at seventy cents a crack and this little bit of shit has been selling them around my patch at sixty five cents. Listen to me you pack of amateurs. Don't think you can come over to London and fuck about with the professionals."

Jamsey began to feel a bit more relaxed. "Hold on, mate, hold on. We can work something out here. Bobo there is just a wanker, I'm the boss around here, and we can cut a deal. Just calm down, mate, Okay?"

Bobo was still lying on the floor and Gary was holding his head in his arms.

He looked up at the main Brit and said, "He's badly hurt. Let me take him over to the hospital, it's just across the road."

The Brit said, "Fuck off. Let him lie there." Then he started to rant and rave about how he had bought moody dollars from contacts in Birmingham just to find out he was being undercut by 'this little fuck'.

Jamesy raised his hands again and said, "Listen here, mate. Somebody has got their wires crossed. Look, I can give you all the dollars you need at the right money and nobody will undercut you. I can give you my word on that."

Bobo seemed to be drifting in and out of consciousness.

Gary spoke up again, "Look, let me take him over to the hospital. It's only across the road. This man could die here."

"No"

"Look, if you want a deal you won't get it if this wee man dies."

The Brit looked around and pointed at Brian sitting in front of his dominoes. "Okay, that old boy over there can take him to the hospital, but no one else leaves after that until we're gone." Old Brian went over to Bobo and helped him to his feet. Bobo looked like he was completely gone and was pleading to the English men not to hit him again.

"Please, I'm so sorry." he said as he was led out of the club by Brian.

As soon as they stepped out onto the Grosvenor Road the dejected and pathetic Bobo suddenly came to life, slapped Brian on the back and said, "Listen here, mucker. Go you on home and make yourself a wee cup of tea and don't come out for a good few hours, or better still stay in for the rest of the night."

Old Brian was amazed at the miraculous recovery.

Bobo got to work right away. He went straight to his house in Clonard Street, out to the back yard and pulled back his wheelie bin. There was a loose concrete slab were the bin had been. He lifted the slab and pulled out a large plastic box that had been concealed under it. Another one was packed in just below that. *Bobo had never decommissioned.* He had little boxes of tricks planted everywhere around Belfast and one or two well greased and packed weapons, mostly handguns and a machine pistol. He always thought, *you never know when you are going to need a bit of gear*.

He took the plastic box into his small living room. Then he went to a cupboard and took out two nine volt radio batteries and pulled the clear plastic wrapping off them. One of the batteries was placed into a small remote control pad. He opened the box which contained seven pounds of Semtex, the rudder mechanism for a remote controlled model airplane and two low tension electric detonators.

He worked fast, only stopping to wipe the blood that was running down the back of his ear. He checked the rudder and could see it was working. He placed a piece of plastic between the two contact points and quickly connected the detonators and stuck the caps into the explosives.

Meanwhile Jamesy had been dishing up free drink to his newfound business partners. Three of the five cockneys had served in Belfast with the Green Jackets and so knew where to find Bobo when they heard that the Official IRA was involved. They also had contacts in the Loyalist gangs who'd supplied them with their weapons. Jamesy had taken phone numbers and the name of their local pub in London and told them it would be a pleasure to do business with them.

The five left the club and went round the corner to their hire car. They got in and the boss was about to switch the engine on. He heard a shout that came from behind him.

"Hey, big shite!"

The Englishman put the window down and looked down the street.

"Hey, mister professional. Have some of this."

When he saw Bobo with the remote control the Englishman knew right away what it was.

"Fucking hell, no!" He grabbed at the door handle.

Bobo flicked the switch as he stepped back into the doorway that he had been waiting in.

Looked like Jamesy's new deal had fallen through.

Danny was back in Moscow again, this time alone. He was going to meet Yang once again and pay for more Dollars. He had changed his passport and had arranged for two sleepers to take the money on a flight the day before.

They were booked into a small hotel not far from the Korean embassy and waited for Danny to get in touch. Danny was to meet Yang at six o'clock. It was only one, so he decided to do a dry run from the small hotel to the embassy and scout the place. He had brought a camera with him to give him the look of a tourist. He also wanted to get a few photos anyway.

He walked down to Rameskin towards the embassy, as he turned a corner he couldn't believe what he was seeing. Yang was in the street about four blocks away from the embassy. He was standing at the back of a large black van and was just closing the back door, but not before Danny caught sight of the silver packing cases that the paperwork came to the embassy in.

Yang went to the driver's door as it opened. If Danny thought this was strange what happened next almost blew him away. The same American who had raided his hotel room in Bulgaria jumped from the van and Yang shook hands with him before climbing into the driver's seat. Danny got a perfect shot with his camera of the transaction. As Yang drove off towards the embassy a large black Mercedes pulled up and the American got in. Danny turned and looked into a shop window as the Mercedes came towards him. As the car passed him Danny turned and clicked his camera at the Merc' and got a side face shot of the American Agent. Danny was completely confused and dismayed at what he had just seen.

He went back to the small hotel and got the money from his two carriers. As usual he took the money from the suitcases and put it into two large sports bags. He waited in the lounge of the hotel for Anton. He arrived at ten minutes to six and he and Danny carried the two bags of sterling out to Anton's jeep. Two of Anton's ex-KGB men were standing at the car and got in to the back seat while Danny and Anton got into the front. They drove to the embassy and the two bodyguards stayed in the jeep while Danny and Anton went inside. Yang greeted them as usual and took the money from them. He showed them the dollars that were allocated to them.

Danny went over to the table that the boxes of paperwork were on. He lifted the lid of one of them and as he did Yang spoke up in a rather different tone than his usual confident and authoritative voice.

"You will note a difference in the paperwork, Danny. This is the new American FRN."

Danny couldn't believe what he was looking at. The notes in the jacket he lifted out were the new design, the new big head note.

Danny looked at Yang and said, "How did your people do this Yang? These notes haven't even hit the streets yet."

"We have our methods Danny but do not worry about such matters. All you need to do is carry on with your good work. Where shall we bring your dollars to this time Danny?"

Danny took a few moments to get his head around everything and then snapped out of it.

"Oh right. Right, well, I've organised twelve people to come with me to a skiing resort in Romania."

"Yes, that is good we have good contacts there. It will be no problem to get the paperwork to you in Romania, you will need another weapon?" Asked Yang.

"I will, Yang, yes. A TT33 will be appreciated."

Danny gave Yang the details of the hotels and a place where he would meet Yang's men to collect the paperwork. Before he left, Danny took five Jackets from one of the boxes and put it into his bag. It was to pay Anton for services rendered. Yang agreed to let Danny take the new notes but warned Anton not to try to change them for another two weeks, which confirmed to Danny that the big heads hadn't even been issued yet.

Sean picked Danny up outside arrivals at Dublin Airport.

"Well, how did it go, Danny?" Sean asked.

"Sean, I don't know what the hell is going on here. The next batch of paperwork we are getting is the new big head notes. Now how did they manage to do that? On top of that, the Yank who turned me over in Bulgaria is working for Yang. I spotted Yang taking a delivery of the paperwork from him. What is going on, Sean?"

Sean said nothing for a moment or so then he started to speak slowly. "Danny, there has been speculation that the paperwork wasn't coming from North Korea at all. There are people who think that the CIA is actually printing the stuff. Now I never believed for a moment that there could be any truth in it, but what you have just told me casts a different light on things, I have to think this thing out and talk to Cathal about it."

"It doesn't make sense. Why would the CIA be at this craic? And how would Yang even stomach dealing with them? He hates the Yanks."

"Danny, the CIA is a law on to its self. They answer to no one and if it furthers their objectives they will do it. As for Yang, I've known him for years and he will deal with anybody. He probably looks at it like this, if the American Agencies want to wage war with each other then let them. The CIA has the Secret Service riddled with their own agents and that is how it would be possible for them to get their hands on the new notes so quickly. That's just my thoughts on the matter, whether it's the case or not, I don't know."

Danny still found it hard to take it all in. Sean left Danny back home to Belfast and both sat very quietly all through the journey.

"What happens next then, Sean?"

"Well, I'll tell Cathal what you have told me. But to be honest, Danny, as far as I'm concerned it's going to be business as usual. So get cracking with the Romanian trip."

"Dead on, Sean. By the way, I got a couple of photos of the whole thing. I'll let you see them when I get them developed."

Sean drove down to the Workers and met up with Gary. He wanted him to go to Belarus with him to help put the finishing touches to the timber lorry operation. Sean wanted to get the last of the small heads over to Ireland and get them changed before Danny brought the new big heads back from Romania.

It was the second week in December and Danny, Bobo and five couples had arrived in the ski resort of Poianna Brasov in Romania. It was something similar to the Bulgarian trip, only freezing. Not one from the party could ski and they had the same instructions to pretend they did not know each other. Bobo had restarted the London boys and found out who grassed him up to the Cockney Gangsters. He organised a good beating for the informer before he returned from London in time to go with Danny.

Whispered conversations in the pubs in London about the fate of the professionals who went to Belfast and did not come back did two things; it got the Belfast men a hell of a lot more respect, and it frightened the shit out of the wise guys in the Gangsters Bar who disappeared overnight and changed their phone numbers.

So the Westies had to do a lot of the donkey work themselves. Lucky enough, Bobo had set the op up well, and Mark and Chomper were looking after things and getting a better return for the dollars. Mark brought the paperwork over to the Halloway Road on Monday and by Thursday or Friday it was all changed and ready for Mark to collect. Tony was sometimes annoyed to come home from work to the sight of Mark counting thousands of pounds cash and sticking it under the floor boards. Mark had not worked or cooked since the op started and he and Tony were getting very fat due to the fact they were now eating out every night at the Greeks or the Indian. Tony made sure that Mark kept receipts and an explanation as to why they were spending Sean McStravick's money.

The Skiers landed in Bucharest airport and the transfer coach took them the one hundred and eighty km trip to Poiana Brasov ski resort in the Carpathian Mountains. Danny was totally stunned by the scenery as they travelled the mountain roads. They arrived in the resort around four in the afternoon and each of the couples separated and went to their respective hotels.

They all arrived at the nursery slopes around nine thirty the next morning to start their Skiing lessons. They were hopeless.

Danny had spent nearly two grand on skiing gear. They could have hired skis in the resort, but that would have meant they had no reason to take ski bags with them which was the whole idea of the trip, more room for the paperwork. Now he knew that no one could ski, and it looked like the equipment was going to go back to Ireland after hardly touching the snow. Danny was pissed with the idea and went around the hotels telling the couples they needed to at least try to ski, and anyway it was a good reason to talk to each other if they were all in the same skiing classes. This made it easier to keep in touch with everyone.

Danny was a crap skier too. He spent most of the ski lessons on his arse, as did most of the others. Some did a little better, but Bobo! Bobo was sailing down the pistes like a pro after the first lesson. Unknown to Danny, it was because he was half drunk.

On the third day Danny gave up, but he ordered everyone else to stick it out. It would be too noticeable if nearly all the skiing class disappeared at once and this way Danny could spend a day getting to know his way around the Romanian resort before he met up with Yang's men.

It was the day before the skiers were to leave for Dublin and Danny had been busy. He had hired a car and drove down from the mountain ski resort twenty miles towards Bucharest and found an old wood mill. He got in touch with Yang and gave him directions to the mill and a meeting time.

Danny was nervous after what he had seen in Moscow and he picked the meeting place carefully. He had a point on high ground were he could watch the entrance to the mill through a small pair of binoculars and an escape route he could use if he saw anything suspicious.

He had parked the car in a fire break in the forest above the mill and watched Yang's men drive in. He could see it was the same pair he had met in Bulgaria and felt a bit more at ease. He waited a few more minutes and after satisfying himself that all looked sweet he jumped into the car and drove down to the timber mill.

"Hello comrade, Danny." the agent in charge said, as Danny pulled up and got out of the car. He went over to the North Korean and shook hands.

"You get around, my friend." Danny said.

Yang's agent bowed slightly and said, "As you do too, comrade." And let go of Danny's hand.

Danny nodded to the agent who was riding shotgun and was barely acknowledged with a slight movement of the eyes and an almost unrecognisable nod.

"I have done the same again, Danny," the agent said smiling. He took Danny to the car to show him the suitcases full of paperwork. "There are five suitcases, each with three million American dollars."

Danny had asked for an extra million per couple as it was going to be easy to place the paperwork in among the skiing gear and the half empty suitcases. They both took the paperwork from the Korean's car to Danny's and packed it into the boot and the back seats. After again shaking hands they both left the saw mill.

Danny got back to the resort just in time as it had started to snow and at the best of times the old Eastern Bloc car was hard to control even though the roads in the resort were cleared by the local authorities. Danny made his way round the five hotels and met up with the couples. He went with them to their rooms with the paperwork. Unlike Bulgaria, the hotels were smaller and he could not just walk in and out of other peoples rooms unnoticed, so this time the couples accompanied him.

The first four couples, when they saw the dollars, were happy enough with the status quo. They actually thought they were carrying heavier stuff than fake dollars. But the fifth couple buckled. The sight of three million in the case first off, panicked the husband, and then the wife freaked out after looking at the panic on her man's face.

"No way, no way," was all the woman would say as the husband kept apologising to Danny and saying they couldn't do it.

Danny eventually gave up with the couple and took the case back down to his car and threw it in. He drove to his own hotel and stopped on the way at an outdoor pursuits shop where he purchased a water proof utility bag and a plastic ground sheet. He also grabbed a can of synthetic grease. He chose the bag well, explaining to the Romanian sales man that he would be storing important equipment in it, in wet conditions.

Danny met up with Bobo who was sitting in the cosy lounge in front of the fire. He actually had a healthy look about him due to his time on the piste and the fact that he was coming back to his hotel and going to bed exhausted every evening instead of drinking all night. Danny told him what was happening and explained what he was going to do.

Danny went down to the ski room in the basement of the hotel. He had noticed that there were shovels, picks and other gardening equipment down there earlier in the week. Bobo went down with him and they grabbed a pick and two shovels. They went out the door of the ski room which led out directly to the car park and went to Danny's car. They threw the tools into the boot and jumped in.

Danny took the car out of the resort and down the same side road that led to the main Bucharest Road then a mile or so before the intersection he pulled into a parking area.

The car park was for mountain walkers and hikers in the summer months and was at the bottom of a forested area of the mountains. Danny and Bobo got out of the car. There was not a sinner in sight, Danny went round to the car boot and took the paperwork from the suitcase and put it into the water proof utility bag . He took out the TT33 which had been in his belt since Yang's men had given it to him, and quickly smeared it all over with synthetic grease and put it into a jiffy bag. He placed the gun in with the paperwork.

Between them they took the pick, shovels, the ground and the waterproof bag stuffed with dollars and the gun and went scrambling up the mountain through the forest fire breaks. After fifteen minutes Danny told Bobo to follow him out of the fire break and into the fir trees. They went deep into the forest where the snow didn't lie due to the fact that they were further down the mountain and the trees kept the ground that bit warmer. Danny was glad that not only was there no snow but also there was a carpet of dead pine needles about nine inches thick lying on the forest floor.

After taking note of exactly where he stood, he carefully lifted arms full of pine needles and gently set them to the side. Bobo had been standing about ten feet to his left holding the tools and thinking Danny had lost it, as he watched him on his knees moving the pine needles. When Danny had cleared an area of about eight foot square he nodded at Bobo.

"All right, Eddie the Eagle, start digging."

Bobo and Danny dug the hole between them. Danny had put the plastic sheet on the ground and the excavated earth was stacked on it. When they had finished digging Danny dropped the bag down into the hole and blew it a kiss. It took the two of them about ten minutes to fill the hole in on top of the bag. Bobo stood shivering in the Romanian winter chill.

"Look, see you Danny Dee, you must hate me. One week I'm getting the arse roasted off me and then the next I'm freezing my balls off." Danny laughed and said, "Right, muscles, give me a lift with this."

They took two corners each and lifted the plastic sheet and carried it further into the forest and then scattered the excess earth around a spot that was covered in shrubbery and young trees. They went back to where the cash was buried and Danny told Bobo to stand back from the covered in hole, he then used his right forearm to spread the pile of pine needles over the upturned ground.

Danny then went to one of the pine trees and started to gently break off dead branches. He took them over to the spot two at a time, he held them out at arm's length and hit them together. The dead needles showered down over the treasure trove, he repeated this about ten times and then backed away still spreading the dead needles over his foot prints. By the time Danny had backed his way to the fire break it looked like no one had set foot in that part of the forest for years.

Bobo watched Danny's every move he was amazed at his expertise.

"How long were you in Vietnam then, big lad?"

Danny laughed "I could have taught the Viet Cong a thing or two," he said proudly.

They got back to the resort just before dark and went to their hotel. Danny was happy with the way he had handled things and knew that Sean would agree with him. It was the best way to take care of the emergency. They could arrange another ski trip and bring an extra pair of hands the next time. They went up to their room and went in. Bobo flopped down on one of the beds with his hands behind the back of his head.

"Right, Bobo, you have earned yourself a good drink tonight. We fly home tomorrow and we are going home with twelve million. Only another forty or so to make the one hundred million Sean is looking for, and it's twelve million big heads, not those aul shite small heads we've been busting our balls with."

"Here Danny, see these big heads that the Yanks are printing now? Do you think they got the idea for them from you, ye big headed shite ye?"

Danny threw a kick in Bobo's direction and went to the shower.

Bobo shouted, "Don't use all the hot water."

When Danny got out of the shower Bobo was fast asleep.

Danny got dressed and decided to take a walk up through the small village resort. While visiting the lively après ski bars, he came across four of the couples in one of the them, they were having a ball, not too drunk, but enjoying the craic, and Danny was all right with that. The couple who had backed down were not to be seen and Danny was also happy with that but he had a niggling feeling that he was being watched so he stayed on his own all night and went back to the hotel after an hour or so.

Next morning Danny and Bobo enjoyed a hearty breakfast and waited for their transfer coach. They took their bags down stairs and it wasn't long before they were on the coach headed for the airport. No problems everything was sweet and the five couples collected their luggage in Dublin Airport and went out side to take their taxis to swords.

Reggie had hired a van this time because he knew that there would be ski bags thrown in and his family car wouldn't take five sets of ski bags and five suitcases. Gary did his job with the mini bus but there was no celebration this time due to the couple who bottled out. They all got back to Belfast safely and Reggie and Mick Rogers got the twelve million well planked.

Gary left the five couples off at the Workers and the bottled out couple slinked off home. The other four couples where in a cheerful enough mood they knew they had done a good job and three of the couples would be accepting their kick back while the other couple were happy that they contributed to the cause.

Danny, Bobo and the rest demanded a free bar for the rest of the night from Gary. He was just about to deny such a request then seen the look that Danny fired at him and said to the money smugglers, "Free drink all night." Yahoo!

Danny and Bobo also enjoyed a bit of the night but had to listen to Gary tell them a dozen times how he and Sean had brought in twenty million in the Belarus timber lorry. The Belarus op was the last of the small heads and Sean wanted them changed as quickly as possible before they started to change the new big heads. Over the next three weeks Bobo and Danny worked flat out, Danny meeting Anton in Birmingham and Bobo working with the Westies in London. It wouldn't be long before they would be ready to start with the big heads. Sean told Danny to set up another Romanian trip and to collect the three million he had buried along with another batch from Yang.

Chapter 10

It was two weeks before Christmas, and Danny sat at Bronagh's side in the delivery room of the maternity suite in the Royal Hospital. He was proudly holding his newborn baby son. He held him up to the window to let the girls see him. Danny had put the next Romanian trip off, until after Christmas as he wouldn't leave Bronagh so soon after the birth. He left his wife and went out to the two over excited girls and took them to the ice cream shop before heading home.

He had just settled the girls in bed for the night when an almighty crash broke the peaceful setting of the house.

He ran downstairs and was met by two cops. They had kicked the front door in and were standing in the middle of the sitting room guns at the ready. More cops were pouring in and going through the house searching. He ran back up the stairs to assure the girls that everything would be all right. The two cops ran up the stairs and grabbed Danny. He told them to take it easy he would go quietly he just needed to get the next door neighbour to come in and look after the children.

They took him back downstairs and one of the cops went next door and got the woman of the house. She told Danny not to worry that she would look after everything. The cops cuffed Danny and took him out to the armoured Land Rover they had arrived in.

He was taken to Castlereagh Interrogation Centre where he was formally charged with the armed robbery of the Newry Post Office. The CID officers questioned him about many other operations but Danny did what he was trained to do. He sat through every interview without uttering a word.

In the middle of the last interview he had a strange visit. The two CID men left the room and in came his old friend, the American who he had seen in Bulgaria and with Yang in Moscow.

"Well Danny, you're in the shit now. Your new son will be what, twenty, twenty-five, before he sees you outside of jail?"

Danny said nothing.

"Danny, I can make this go away for you. My people have a strong influence with the Northern Ireland Police and the Judiciary. I don't have to tell you what we want, you know what we want, McStravick, Sean McStravick. We need him placed with a large amount of paperwork. Yes, we know all about your methods and terms. McStravick is the man we want and we will get him with or without your help. The two officers outside can contact me when you get some sense and start talking to us."

He left the room and the CID came back in to take him to his cell and on the way one of them said "You must be some sort of a kingpin, Devine, to get a visit from that guy."

Danny's lawyer explained to him the evidence that they had against him was three characteristics of the finger print on his right forefinger. With the wrong judge it would be just enough to convict him, and if convicted he would be looking at fifteen to twenty maybe even twenty-five.

The Northern Ireland judiciary was running on overdrive, the amount of cases that was coming through was threatening to grind the system to a standstill. The top cops had come to an unwritten agreement with the top judges. Okay decide the sentencing on cases that were going to drag on and offer deals. It was horse trading between the cops the prosecution and the defence lawyers. At that time a defence lawyer would have known how long his client was going to get before his trial began.

The prosecution were looking for a full trial and to stick the *Cowboy Robber* away for twenty; they knew by the description of Danny's Webley just how many jobs he had pulled. The judge knew just how smart and how confident Danny was, and worked out just what he would accept when offered a deal.

"Four years, four fucking years," the cops and the prosecution were almost in tears, "he gets out in two."

The learned judge in all his wisdom and experience told the cops and the prosecution lawyers, "Look I know what he will take, I know what he deserves and it is a lot more than I am going to give him. If he fights it he could win and walk, so that's it. Kiss my ass if you don't like it. Now you can fuck off and cry your eyes out for as long as you like, but I am going to the golf club and I better get a memo on my desk next Tuesday that Daniel Devine was sentenced to four years imprisonment on the Fourteenth of December Nineteen Ninety Six, after pleading guilty to armed robbery. Anyway I kind of like this guy," he said, much to the chagrin and wrath of everyone assembled.

The horsebox took Danny from the remand wing to the High Court in Belfast, as he was being led down to the cells below the court he and his guards were stopped in one of the long corridors by none other than the American agent; the guards were taken by surprise at the presence of the man. He flashed a badge at them but they still looked confused.

The Yank said quickly, "Danny boy, if you don't deal with us now you are going down for twenty years. It's your choice."

For the first time Danny spoke to his nemesis. "Listen, you big fuck, if I get one day over four years, see the photos I have of you and Yang in Moscow, well those photos go to the papers, shortly after they will go to the Secret Service, also... I will find you and I will kill you." The Yank laughed, but Danny could sense it was a nervous laugh.

"What photos? You have no photos."

Danny did his time, bad times and good times. Good visits from Bronagh and bad visits from Bronagh. The baby boy, Daniel, said "Mama," the girls got medals for Irish dancing, gran' and granddad came up and took us all out for the day in Newcastle and so on.

Bronagh had very little money and even though Gary was doing his best, the movement were not being too helpful. Unknown to everyone it was Jamesy who was putting the brakes on any financial help going her way. Bobo was stood down after Danny's arrest thanks to Jamesy and could not do much for Bronagh, although every second Tuesday an envelope with ten quid was mysteriously pushed through the letter box.

The time passed quickly, Danny would be released in four weeks time. The mortgage company were in the process of taking the house off Bronagh. She knew that Danny was going to get out before the final act and she hoped that he could do something to save the day.

Danny Devine was released on the Fifteenth of December 1998. He had received his full remission of fifty percent of the four year sentence. He was not a happy camper. He wanted to kick the crap out of Jamesy and then go down to GHQ to find out why his family had not been looked after while he was inside but he had decided on a different direction. There was three million big head dollars in Romania and they belonged to him. Fuck the Revolution and the same to Socialism; no one looked after mine and me so I will look after myself.

Danny came out of the gates of Maghaberry Prison and was greeted by Bronagh, the kids and Bobo.

"Okay, you lot," Danny declared as the girls came running towards him. He had a mixture of emotions, his love for Bronagh and his three children, the hatred he had for the movement that let him down and almost let his family be evicted from their home, and then the touch of freedom and the feeling that nothing else matters. Also for a minute the feeling of true friendship that he and Bobo shared.

Then back to the movement. Bronagh had struggled for two years to keep the kids and the house running smoothly. Gary had told Sean they needed help and Sean had always sent word up to Jamesy to make sure that Bronagh was looked after. Jamesy had a different story for Gary. His story was more along the lines that he would do what he could. He would help out a bit, but the movement was running out of money again and the prisoners and their families had to try to look after themselves. Bronagh was too proud to complain to her father, and she did not want to look like she was a beggar and so it went on that Bronagh was getting no help and Gary thought she was.

Bronagh stepped up to Danny and kissed him hard on the lips. The kids giggled and Bobo turned away. Baby Daniel wondered why it was so much warmer all of a sudden and why he could not move his arms whicht were pinned between these two giants.

"Right," Danny said, "Chinese, Indian or fish and chips, come on what's it going to be?"

Bronagh threw her head back, "How dare you say that? Straight home to a good feed."

The grub was lovely. Two big fat juicy roast chickens, stuffing, mashed potatoes, a lake of gravy and loads of tinned marrowfat peas. Gary and Eileen had made their way to the house and joined in the celebrations. Danny was just over the moon to be back in his wee home along with his family. Bobo got drunk as a skunk and phoned for a taxi around one o'clock am. Gary and Eileen stayed the night, Eileen slept in with the girls and Gary on the couch.

They all got up early the next morning and Bronagh was a bit peeved as she thought there was a chance of a bit of romance on their first night together but it didn't happen. Gary and Eileen assured them they would have the house to themselves later as they were going to look after the three kids that night. Before Gary left he told Danny that he needed to talk to Sean and get something sorted out about the three million in Romania. He had sent Bobo over e few times to try to find the money but Bobo could never seem to pinpoint the cash, however he did always seem to have a hell of a good time looking for it.

A week or so after Danny's release Sean made arrangements for a meeting. He and Danny met in the Celtic Club Bar. Danny was still seething over the way Bronagh had been treated.

Sean walked into the bar and extended his hand to Danny who refused to take it. Sean was puzzled. "What's wrong with you Danny, what's wrong?" "What's wrong?" My wife was treated like shite the whole time I was inside, that's what's wrong." Sean did not know how to react, he had told Jamesy to make sure that Bronagh was looked after but he did not want to say anything until he had the full facts, he asked Danny to let him look into what had happened. Then Sean done the worst thing he could have done, he brought up the business of the three million still buried in Romania.

That was it for Danny he sat quietly listening to Sean and told him there was no problem he would arrange to go out and dig it up for the movement. But inside he had decided, no, no that money was his, that money was compensation for two lost years of freedom, and hardship for his wife and kids.

It was a new age in terrorism. Rumours of extremist Muslims were hot and airports were now like fortresses. Nothing was going through undetected and Danny knew it. Sean only needed the money recovered in Romania and he could then get it back to Ireland through Belarus.

Danny went to Dublin the next day. Sean had given him funding for the Romanian trip, a bit of spending money, and the money for a fake passport, Danny went to see Joxer in a bar in Talbot Street. Danny didn't mind dealing with Joxer he was a likeable rogue. Danny waited in the bar for an hour before his passport arrived and he paid up. Gary had made the booking to Romania the week before and Danny was due to fly out in five days.

On the morning of the flight Gary called to Danny's house to take him to the airport, he wanted to assure Bronagh that Danny would not be doing anything that would get him time, or get him hurt.

As they left the house Gary stopped for a second and said to Danny I know you're not going to like this but Sean told us to send two of the guys along with you. Jamesy got to pick them; it's Luke and big Marty Brown. Danny was furious and also very suspicious but he held his tongue and said nothing. They got to the airport Danny checked in. The two big mates were booked separately from Danny and checked in on their own.

When they arrived in Romania they collected their luggage and went out side to the transfer coach. They also sat apart during the trip to Poiana. When they got to the resort they went to their hotels. The two hotels where just down the street from each other and as they stood together and waited for their cases to come off the coach, Danny whispered to Luke.

"Over there tomorrow morning eight o'clock."

He pointed at a small car park beside a wooden chalet. Luke nodded. Danny spent the rest of the day hiring a car and getting shovels and a pick he also bought himself a large haversack. He didn't sleep too well that night. A thousand things were going around in his brain at once. He drifted in and out of sleep from time to time before eventually getting up for breakfast at seven thirty.

Danny went out into the crisp air and breathed deeply, it helped a little. He could see the two big Belfast thugs trundling along towards the meeting point.

He got into the hire car and drove over to meet them. There were very few people around as the ski lifts didn't open until eight thirty. The two massive men got into the car and Danny headed out of the resort towards Bucharest. Danny said nothing on the journey to the buried money. He despised the pair of thugs; in fact no one liked them. Their own families didn't even like them. They had both been divorced for years and the only company they ever kept was each other's.

After driving for a half hour they arrived at the forest car park and Danny spoke for the first time.

"Here, take these. We're heading up there along those trails up the side of the mountain." He handed them each a shovel and started up along the fire breaks.

"Is it far?" Marty whined.

Danny looked round at him and just said, "C'mon," nodding towards the high ground in front of them.

Danny laughed to himself. After a long climb they got to the clearing and Danny was still taking great pleasure at the sight of the two big gobshites struggling for breath and crying about aching legs and muscles. Danny found the spot right away after counting the paces from the tree he had marked, but deliberately started to dig a foot or so to the side of where the bag was placed. They dug in turn for about three hours as the hole got deeper the two boys started complaining and questioning if he had the right spot.

Danny had taken his third turn at digging and knew he was well past the box it was only a matter of digging into the side of the hole. Luke had gone over to a tree to relieve himself and Marty was sitting on a large rock, half asleep.

Danny made his move. He dug into the side of the hole and after a few strikes with the shovel he could see the bag. He scraped away more earth and then pulled hard on the bag dislodging it. He opened the bag and pulled out the TT33 and slid a round into the chamber. It took him all his strength to throw the bag up out of the hole.

The noise of the bag landing made Marty look up. Danny clambered out of the hole just as Luke was coming back. Marty had got to his feet and Luke gave him a nod. Almost simultaneously the two thugs slid extendable metal batons from their sleeves. The batons opened with a metallic click. The duo started towards Danny, Marty with a sneaky grin on his face.

"Nothing personal, Danny. Just orders"

The two huge men were twice the size of Danny and would have no problem beating him to death. Danny could have run but he wasn't leaving the money. He was holding the TT33 behind his back.

"This *is* personal," he said as he fired two snap shots into the chests of the two would be killers -- big chests big targets.

They fell in a heap together on the ground, both died instantly. Danny went to work right away. He dragged the two bodies one at a time with great effort, to the edge of the hole. He searched the both of them and took their hotel room key and their IDs before tipping both bodies into the shallow grave. Because he hadn't used a ground sheet it took him longer to disguise the excavation. He eventually got it looking all right and started down from the forest. On the way down he hid the tools as he had no further use for them. He got to the car park just as it began to get dark.

He loaded the bag of paperwork into the boot of the hire car and headed back to the resort and went to the thug's hotel first, he knew that all the hotels where similar and he entered through the ski room and up the back stairs to the bed rooms. The room number was on the key and he got in before any one seen him.

He gathered up Martin and Luke's belongings. There was writing paper on a desk in the room and Danny scribbled out a note using his left hand to write it. It explained that they didn't like the skiing and had decided to go on a tour of Romania, they said they would be travelling around for a couple of weeks and would make their own way back to Ireland.

Danny put the note into an envelope and addressed it to the holiday company rep. He took their belongings and went round to his own hotel. Behind his hotel there were three big dumpsters. He removed about ten full rubbish sacks and threw the thugs belonging into the dumpster and lobbed the rubbish sacks back in on top of them.

He then went back round to the front of the hotel and went up stairs to his own room and packed leaving a similar note for the company rep. Danny was buying time before a missing person alert went out.

The receptionist spotted Danny leaving and was puzzled when she noticed his cases. He went over to her and gave her his room key and the note.

Danny shrugged his shoulders and said, "I just can't get the hang of this skiing so I've met up with another two Irish men and we've decided to go touring around Romania. Can you explain that to the rep? Here's a note for her anyway."

The receptionist took the key and the note and said she would look after things. She also said how sorry she was that he did not like the skiing.

Danny went over to the car; he opened the boot and transferred the paperwork from the soiled bag into the big rucksack. He took a few changes of clothes from his cases and threw them on top of the paperwork. He took the cases and the bag round to the dumpsters and repeated the same routine with the rubbish covering his own luggage.

Danny took the hire car to the office which was closed so he put the keys through the letter box. He walked down the street to the taxi rank. A taxi arrived a few minutes later. After putting the rucksack into the boot he got in and the taxi driver took off.

Danny had earlier collected timetables and maps of the railway system in Romania and a good map of Europe from the Tourist Office. He told the driver to take him to the station in Brasov. This cut out the long trip to Bucharest. In Brasov he could pick up on the Bucharest to Budapest train. He would have to change trains at Oradea a city on the Hungarian border. The taxi took him to the train station where he bought his ticket. He sat in a small all night café beside the platform and waited, spending most of his time working out his best route to France. The Budapest train arrived at two thirty am the next morning and Danny boarded. It was the start of a long journey across two Eastern Bloc and three Western European countries.

On the train Danny slept from time to time and was asleep when the train reached Oradea at six thirty am. He got off and got the connection to Budapest within an hour. There was a lot of security around the station as it was the last stop before they left Romania and entered Hungary. Danny was nervous. He knew if he was stopped and searched in one of the two the Eastern Bloc countries the dollars would simply disappear and he would be thrown into jail for years without a trial. He was sweating. But he boarded the train without incident, looked just like any one of the many backpackers in the station. Sweat over.

The Hungarian train was slightly more comfortable than the Romanian one and there was a dining car. He had breakfast there and after bringing him the tray, the waiter advised him in broken English to adjust his watch by one hour as they had just entered Hungary.

The train arrived at the main Keleti station in Budapest at four thirty pm and Danny got off, he was completely knackered. Security was similar in the Hungarian station as it was in Oradea. But he again blended in as a backpacker. He had no Hungarian currency so he found a change bureau in the station and changed his Romanian Leu for Hungarian Forint.

His next step on the journey was to go to Austria, and he could see on the information boards there was a train leaving for Vienna within the hour but Danny wasn't interested. He wanted a good night's sleep.

Across the road from the main entrance of the station was a small hotel. It beckoned to Danny. The hotel was basic but cheap, there was hot water and a comfortable bed. After checking in he went upstairs and had a shower in the bathroom situated in the corridor were his room was. He took his rucksack into the bathroom with him and after a change of clothes in his bedroom. He went downstairs to the dining room for the evening meal. He still had the rucksack with him. He slept with it in his arms that night.

Next morning Danny got up had breakfast and checked out. He went back into the train station and was glad to find he had only twenty minutes to wait for a train to Vienna. He bought his ticket and before long he was on his way to Austria and getting closer to France and better still closer to Rosin Dubh. The Dark Rosaleen that is Ireland.

The train journey was pleasant and Danny was pleased he would soon be back in Western Europe. As they approached the small town of Gyor the train started to slow. This surprised and worried Danny as the train was supposed to be nonstop between the two cities. The train came to a stop in the small station and Danny could see four Hungarian police men get on the train before it resumed the journey. The sweat was back on.

The police started at the back of the train and started to slowly make their way up through the carriages. Danny thought his luck was about to run out. It was twenty minutes since the police had boarded and they were just two carriages behind him. Danny had finished the one hundred and forty second Hail Mary when the train started to slow. It stopped at the border town of Hegyeshalom and the police got off.

"Holy Mary mother of God. Thank you, thank you, thank you." Danny was almost in tears.

They crossed Austrian border within five minutes and Danny was on a high as the train pulled into Westhoff Station in Vienna.

As the passengers got off and went towards the exit gate from the platform he could see a few men up ahead making random checks on passports. Danny was relieved to see that the checks were carried out on mainly ethnic men and he was waved through at the gate. When he got into the main part of the station he looked for and found a change bureau. He passed four hundred dollars for Austrian Phennigs and then looked for a phone to call Bronagh who just broke down crying with relief.

Danny left the phone booth and looked for the information boards. He couldn't believe his luck. There was an overnight train direct from Vienna to Paris. The Eurotrain inter city service had just started earlier in the year. It was expensive but Danny didn't care. He thought he had another three days travelling in front of him. He phoned Bronagh again to give her the good news. The train would leave at eight thirty pm and be in Paris the next morning at around ten thirty: fourteen hours, what a gift.

Danny bought his ticket and confirmed the times with the ticket clerk and then went outside into the fresh air to kill a few hours.

The train was amazing. It made the Belfast to Dublin Enterprise look like a bone shaker. Danny had paid for a private double cabin and the first thing he did when he got into it was to strip off and wash from head to foot.

He had earlier bought himself two complete changes of clothes and underwear. He also bought a new jacket. As he changed he enjoyed the crisp clean feel of the new shirt on his skin. He threw all his old clothes into the bin.

Danny got into bed around twelve o'clock. He had spent the evening drinking and eating in style, he had plenty of Austrian phennigs to spend and he was in tip top form. He had the best night's sleep ever and woke at seven thirty. After opening the blinds on the window he lay on top of the bed watching the French countryside go by. The train stopped at Nancy and Danny knew from the schedule it was only three hours before they would get into Paris Est. He got washed and dressed and went down to the dining car for breakfast. He stayed in the dining car for an hour or so after he had finished breakfast and then went down to his cabin to gather up his belongings, he was still clutching his big rucksack, it never left his side all through the journey.

After stepping off the train on to the platform Danny made his way to the main hall. The first thing he saw, was a busy change bureau. Danny went into a booth in the gents toilets and took a jacket out of the paperwork and split it into ten one grand bundles. The station was packed and the teller behind the glass thought nothing of the five thousand dollars that Danny presented, she carried out that type of transaction four or five times a day along with the smaller ones. He asked for two thousand to be changed to French Francs and three into Irish Punts.

Danny went outside and got a taxi to Gare de Nord and done the same at the bureau there. He then went outside and took the bus from Paris to La Harve and waited at the Harbour for the Irish Ferry to come in. As he watched the stream of cars come of the boat mostly filled with families heading off for a Christmas break in France there was also the odd business man. Danny burst out laughing at the site of Bobo driving out of the harbour with his usual worried frown, on top of the fact that he was a crap driver and that he heard he had to drive on the other side of the road when he got to France but he also had drunk the ferry's bar almost dry the night before.

"Jesus, Danny, my head's splitting," Bobo said as he pulled up beside him.

"All right, Bobo?" Danny shouted laughingly. "Good to see you."

Bobo got out of the car and handed Danny the keys. "Here, you can drive from now on. No way am I driving over here. I heard they drove on the right side of the road over here so I tried practising on my way down from Belfast to Rosslare, I'm telling you it was mustard, haaaa." Bobo laughed at his own joke as he punched Danny on the shoulder.

"Ha ha, right, Bobo, we have six hours to kill before the ferry goes back, what about getting a bit of grub, eh?"

"Grub me arse. Where's the nearest pub?"

Everything went smoothly. Danny drove the car down to the big drinks warehouse and parked away from the other cars, he then emptied the rucksack and packed the dollars into the empty spare wheel compartment and said a prayer that they wouldn't get a puncture. He and Bobo went into the warehouse and bought a load of wine and beer stacked it on two trolleys and took them out to the car. They filled the boot full of wine and beer as well as the back seat to make it look like it was just another booze cruise for personal consumption, perfectly legal, and if the customs tested Bobo's alcohol levels they would have no difficulty believing he would consume the lot himself in a week.

Bobo drove back on to the ferry and Danny boarded as a foot passenger carrying his rucksack minus the dollars. Bobo had a cabin booked along with the car so Danny bunked in with him. They got into Rosslare just outside Wexford the next morning. Bobo drove off the boat and through the customs with no trouble. He just had one of those faces that no one took too seriously.

Danny met up with Bobo in the car park and headed for Belfast via Dublin and Newry. They stopped in Newry and changed three grand of the Irish Punts he had got in Paris; he was going to need some sterling. Danny and Bobo arrived in Belfast about five thirty pm. They travelled in the car to the bottom of the M1 motorway and parted company.

When they split up, Danny drove to Twinbrook in South Belfast to a flat that his cousin had let him use while he was working in England, he carried the boxes of wine and beer into the flat, he then took the paperwork from the spare wheel well, put it back in the rucksack and carried that in to the flat, he then gave Bronagh a quick call and went to bed.

After parking the car at the bottom of Broadway Bobo cut through the grounds of the Royal Hospital and walked towards the Grosvenor Road. He came out of the Hospital grounds and crossed the road to the Workers Club, Danny had given him a hundred quid and it was burning a hole in his pocket. He couldn't wait to get into the club for a big pint of cold, cold Guinness. Bobo propped himself up at the bar, after ten minutes or so Gary came in.

"All right, Bobo?" Gary said as he put his hand on Bobo's shoulder.

Bobo turned his head round slightly. "Ach what about you, Gary? Do you want a drink?"

"No you're all right. Any word from Danny? Bronagh is worried sick. He was doing a wee message for Sean and was supposed to be back yesterday but him and two others that were with him haven't showed up."

In fact Bronagh knew exactly what was going on. Danny had phoned and let her know that he was all right and he would be in touch soon. He told her to tell everyone, that she had heard nothing. She was a good actress and knew she had to pretend to everyone, including her own Dad, that she was going out of her mind.

"Well did you hear from him?"

"Not a thing, Doc. Not a bloody thing. I'm worried sick myself." said Bobo.

"Well if you hear anything, let me know. Listen, McStravick is coming up from Dublin the day after tomorrow he wants to see you, so be here for about two, okay?"

"Aye no problem." Bobo said calmly.

He stayed cool but inside his stomach was churning, he knew awkward questions would be asked and worse again he would have to turn up for the meeting completely sober.

Cathal called a meeting with Sean and Mick.

"Well what's the latest, Sean?" Cathal asked.

Sean said there was no sign of them and there is nothing in the papers about any one being arrested at the airports. Jamesy waited for them and the flight came in on time but the boys weren't on it.

"I don't like it. Danny has done something stupid here."

Sean said, "Let's wait and see."

Chapter 11

Danny got up the next morning he showered and shaved. It was the first decent night's sleep since he left Belfast the week before. The journey across Europe in sleeper trains was not for the fainthearted. He cooked up a bit of breakfast and phoned Bronagh. He told her to meet him later in Banbridge, a town twenty miles South of Belfast. Danny told her that Bobo would call up about half seven in the evening, after the kids were in bed and he would stay with them until she got back in the morning. Bronagh didn't like the thought of Bobo babysitting but she just couldn't wait to see Danny again.

Bobo left the light on in his house and sneaked out the back door and up the alley. The Stickies had put somebody on his tail but the boys they sent weren't too bright and he gave them the slip. He went to the Taxi depot on the Springfield Road and got a taxi. He chose this depot because it was run by the Provos, so there was no chance of running into any one he didn't want to see.

The taxi pulled up outside Danny's house and Bobo rapped the door, and waited. Bronagh came to the door dressed and ready to travel. She was holding an overnight bag. Bobo was about to say that Danny told him that she would pay the taxi man. Bronagh walked straight past Bobo, stopping for a split second to warn him not to get drunk. She jumped into the taxi and was heading for the motorway before Bobo had a chance to ask her if there was any thing to drink.

She arrived at the hotel in Banbridge and Danny waited for a second or two before moving. No one had followed her so he jumped out of the car and went over to the taxi. Bronagh got out and threw her arms around Danny.

"Hiya honey," he said to her. "Missed you, but here, let go before you break my back."

He paid the taxi man and led Bronagh over to his car. They got in and headed south towards the border. They crossed the border at Newry and went to the Ballymac Hotel just North of Dundalk.

They checked in, it was a five star hotel and was well out of the budget of any of his ex-comrades so there was little chance of running in to any of them. They went up to their room. When they went in Bronagh thought she would faint at the sight of the luxury. It reminded Danny of the first time he stayed at the Sheraton, for a moment a rush of nostalgic sorrow came over him as he thought of Sean and their lost friendship. He knew things had changed forever.

Danny called down to reception and ordered Champagne to be sent to the room. He also told them they would be dining tonight. The Champagne arrived in a flash. Danny popped the cork and poured. Bronagh came out of the bathroom wearing perfume and nothing else.

"Wow, and we haven't even had the champers yet."

Danny almost fell over as he started pulling his clothes off. Bronagh jumped into the big King size bed and Danny was right behind her.

They went down to dinner and the food was the finest they had ever tasted. Bronagh was having such a lovely time she actually forgot about the kids for a minute or two.

"Well, love, this is it. Things have changed for good there's no going back for me. I've taken what is rightfully mine and I'm keeping it." Danny told Bronagh what had occurred but dodged around the subject of what happened to the other two.

"Bronagh, with this money we can start a new life. Spain, Italy, France we can go anywhere."

Danny told her how much he loved her and the kids and they would have the life they deserved. It all sounded lovely but for one thing, just one thing. If she went with Danny, then she would probably never see her Mum and Dad again, but to Bronagh there was only one decision, Danny and the kids were paramount.

They got up at seven the next morning and Danny took a chance and went to the house. He wanted to see the kids. He was careful as he approached looking all around, but it seemed safe enough. He went into the house and woke the kids and was showered with hugs and kisses. The baby was a bit strange. He was still only two and had not seen much of Danny since he was born.

After the hugs the kids were told to settle down and eat breakfast. Danny went upstairs and dragged Bobo out of bed. He told him to throw his clothes on as quickly as possible. Danny went back downstairs and gave Bronagh two thousand sterling and told her to pay it off the mortgage arrears. Bobo was still trying to get dressed as Danny rushed him out of the house. He was carrying most of his clothes and jumped into the back seat of the car to finish dressing. Danny drove round to the flat in Twinbrook and he and Bobo went in.

"Listen, Danny, when the Stickies realise what has happened here they are going to start looking for you big time. You can't stay around here much longer."

"I've already thought of that, Bobo. I'm going to rent a house somewhere down South out in the countryside and work from there. I'll keep in touch with you. Listen, Bo mate, I need you here with me. The movement is fucked and we need to look after ourselves now."

Bobo shook hands with Danny and said. "Right, right mate, I'll go down to the club and see what I can pick up."

Bobo went down to the Workers, as he went in he felt it didn't hold the same cosy feeling he used to get from it. He thought, maybe it was time to find a new watering hole. Bobo sat at the bar and had a lemonade, that's how bad things had become. Gary and Sean came in and beckoned Bobo to follow them into the back office.

"Bobo, something has gone wrong here. I think Danny may have got his wires crossed and thinks that the movement has let him and Bronagh down. It was more of a breakdown in communication."

Gary cut in, "Sean fuck this. Bobo, you get word to Danny that Jamesy, the stinking cunt, has caused all this. If you hear from him tell him to come in and we will sort it out."

"Now hold on, Gary," Sean said. "We have to investigate all the facts before we start accusing anyone. But you're right, the first thing we need is for Danny to come in and explain what has happened."

Bobo just sat there and shrugged his shoulders, "I haven't heard from him."

Danny had decided on Cavan as a base. It was in the arsehole of nowhere and he knew nobody ever went to it. He drove south from Belfast to Cavan town and visited an estate agent there. He got a list of properties for rent. He told the agent he would take the list away and study it over lunch time. He had told the agent that he had just gone through a messy divorce and was just looking for somewhere that he could move into right away. The agent took the list back and marked out the properties that were available for immediate possession then gave it back to Danny. He left the office and went to a fish and chip shop down the street. He studied the list of properties as he ate his lunch. After two o'clock he went back to the estate agents.

"Listen this one is perfect, the three bed room bungalow with garage. If I can have it right away I am willing to pay a month's rent as a security deposit and three months rent in advance, but I want the keys today."

At two hundred a month that totalled eight hundred punts. The estate agent phoned the owner of the property who told him not to let Danny out of the office and get him signed up right away.

"Oh, and grab the money."

The estate agent gave him the keys after Danny had paid up and shook on it. The estate agent told him to call to the office if he needed to know anything, or if he had any problems.

Danny stayed the night. The house was sat on about two acres of land. It had a few wee tidy gardens round it and the rest of the land just stretched out from the gardens into the fields and then into the countryside.

Next morning Danny awoke and was surprised to find that he had got the heating system set at the right time and that it was working beautifully. After a shower he went out for a walk and picked a spot, way up behind the house where he would make a hide for the paperwork. He went back to the house and got into the car. He headed back across the border towards Armagh. After he had went through Armagh he stopped at a car dealership on the main Armagh Belfast Road. He spoke to a salesman and haggled before he done a deal trading in his old Mondeo and paying two grand to move up three years.

The younger car handled well. For a minute Danny thought about how the old car had served him well, but came back down to earth as he felt the smooth power of the newer car and more important, this car was clean.

Danny got into Belfast and arranged to meet Bobo at the flat. Bobo arrived through a mixture of buses, taxis and leg work. He had started to get paranoid and thought he could see Stickies coming out of the wood work. Bobo rapped the door and Danny let him in.

"Nice wheels, Danny Dee"

"Hiya, Bobo" Danny said. He had already emptied the flat. He had the paperwork, all his belongings and his clothes in the car, he had also loaded the beer and wine into it. After all it would come in handy down in his new country residence. Bobo jumped into the car and they both headed south for Cavan.

Danny and Bobo stayed in the Cavan house that weekend. They drank they sang and they danced.

Monday morning. Danny had been a little lax and kept the paperwork in the house. Now he was walking up the fields with the rucksack on his back. After about ten minutes he came to the small copse he had discovered on Friday. The little tree lined area had a few dry stone walls built inside it and Danny set to work taking them down. He chose a wide and high wall as he knew that after taking away the front stones there would always be large voids behind them.

Before long he had stashed two million superdollars in the wall. He went back to the house and woke Bobo who was not feeling too hot. His head was spinning and he thought that Man United was training in his stomach. Danny eventually got him to drink some coffee and got him out into the car.

"Right, Bo. We're for *Landin ta-day, back ta good al Landin.*"

"No way, Danny Dee, no way. I'm not making that trip today."

Bobo was still protesting as Danny pulled up at Belfast Docks and bought a five day return ticket to Scotland. They got the one o'clock sailing to Stranraer. Danny had packed two hundred grand into the side panels of the boot of the car. He had been very careful taking the panels off and replacing them. They where stopped at security before boarding the ferry but the woman security guard just took a quick look into the boot and asked if they were carrying any extra petrol or firearms.

Down through Mad Mick's Mile they went towards Carlisle, then Danny had a thought he left the main road just as they were about to leave Scotland and turned into Gretna Green. As they pulled into the small town Bobo couldn't believe it.

"Are you serious, Devine? Is this really Gretna Green?"

"Bobo, look at the sign. It says Gretna Green. Tell you what why don't we have our Dinner here?"

They stopped at The Hotel in the village and went in for a slap up feed. After an hour of serious eating they got into the car and went towards Penrith and the M6. They stayed on the Motorways until they reached the old favourite, Watford Gap and booked in to the services hotel.

Next morning they were up at seven and were in London for nine thirty. They parked at Kings Cross in a car park just across from the Tube Station. Danny went to the boot and carefully removed the panels on the side he took out the two hundred thousand and put it to the two small shoulder bags he had bought on Friday in Cavan. With ten jackets in each of the bags they went across the road and down into the Underground. They had bought a couple of three day passes, which meant they could travel anywhere in London. They went to the West End first.

The change bureaus booths were busy and there was almost always an American tourist at the hatch changing dollars. Bobo went first as he was an old hand at this game. He took two Jackets from his bag. He removed the brown tape from them and ruffled them up a bit. He went to the teller behind the glass and threw the dollars into the small compartment below her window. She didn't even look up, she lifted the money out of the small chute and then said, "Passport," as she started counting the dollars.

Bobo dropped his fake passport into the chute and she lifted it out and set it beside the dollars. She did not even look at it as she handed it back to Bobo along with the sterling notes. The exchange rate was criminal and Bobo was just so glad he was giving them shite instead of hard earned cash.

Danny and Bobo went round London all day. They hit a few Banks as well as the bureaus and got a better rate. By three o'clock they had done in the two hundred K. They were both exhausted. They went back to Kings Cross and collected the car and drove North for four hours before leaving the motorway and stopping at a road house for the night.

It was a nice cosy little place just outside Northampton, Danny went to the reception and booked and paid for two single rooms. He just could not face

Bobo's snoring tonight. Bobo had already propped himself up at the bar and had two pints ordered.

Danny came in and said to Bobo. "Listen, I'm wrecked. I'm going straight to bed."

Danny handed Bobo a key for his room and told him he would see him down at breakfast in the morning. Danny was just about to leave to go to his room when Bobo said;

"Here give me a few quid in case I want to buy a drink."

Danny was drifting into sleep as he pulled a bundle of notes from his pocket and was about to pull a few off to give to him, Bobo's hand shot out and grabbed the lot.

"I'll give you you're change back in the morning," Bobo said as he stuck the notes into his shirt pocket.

Danny couldn't be bothered and went on up to bed, he was so tired he didn't see the two hookers at the other end of the bar. The same hookers who were homing in on Bobo now, after the big smile and the wink that he shot at them as soon as Danny left.

Danny went down to breakfast the next morning. He banged on the door of Bobo's room on the way past and was repaid by a muffled, "Go away."

Danny ate a good breakfast and went upstairs to get Bobo up and pack his few belongings. Danny packed his small case and went out of the room. He stopped at Bobo's room and this time eventually got him up. Danny waited out in the corridor as he knew the room would stink of tobacco smoke, smelly feet and farts, what he didn't know that mixed with all that there was also the smell of cheap perfume.

The pair got into the car and rejoined the motorway for Scotland. They reached the port in time for the two thirty afternoon sailing which took them straight into Belfast Port. Danny left Bobo off at a taxi depot in Belfast city centre and gave him a few hundred sterling in case of an emergency. He told him to just show his face around the Falls Road for a day or so.

Bobo went into the Workers that evening, Gary was behind the bar.

"Give me a pint Gary," Bobo said.

Gary stared at Bobo as he pulled the Guinness. "Bobo, tell me. Just tell me he's all right."

"Gary I don't know anything. Honest. But let me tell you something, Danny can look after himself and I'm sure he's all right."

Larkin came out from the back office. He looked at Bobo.

"Where's that fucking mate of yours? Where is he Brannigan"

Bobo looked at him with disdain and continued to drink from his pint. Larkin ran round the counter to grab Bobo by the throat. But Bobo was too quick for him. He threw his drink, glass and all, straight into Larkin's face. The glass cut a gash in Jamesy's forehead and he dropped to his knees as the Guinness mixed with the blood running down Jamesy's face. Bobo got off the stool and walked to the door.

Gary stood behind the bar and didn't move. He just looked at Bobo leaving. Larkin started screaming.

"That's it, Brannigan. Your kneecaps are coming off. I'm going to get you done."

Danny met Bobo in Newry bus station and took him to the house in Cavan. Bobo had stayed in his sister's house the night before, knew he couldn't go back to his own house until the dust settled. Danny laughed when

Bobo told him how he split open Jamesy's forehead with the pint glass of Guinness. They got to the house in Cavan and Bobo went straight to the fridge and pulled two beers out. He handed one to Danny.

"All right, Bobo, just a few tonight. We need to be up fresh and early in the morning." Danny was surprised when Bobo agreed. Danny thought that Bobo seemed worried.

Next morning Danny told Bobo he wanted to do another run to London.

"That's no problem but why don't we do it the old way, and do more?"

"What do you mean?"

"Look our Jim is still doing the fish run to London. If I ask him, he will let us do the business, and better still he will keep his mouth shut."

"Well it's all right getting a load of paperwork over there but we still have to change it ourselves. It's hard work and takes time."

"No! See while you were inside a lot of the boys broke away from the movement. Half the boys in London left and Chomper was one of them. Our Mark and Tony will work for us and I know two of Chomper's mates will give us a hand."

Danny said to Bobo, "Right, we'll do in the rest of the first million. I'll leave the other two for a while. They are safe enough where they are."

Bobo phoned Jim and asked him could he get a lift to London.

Jim said, "No problem. There's a load going out today."

"Bobo can you do this run on your own? I need a bit of time with Bronagh." Danny said.

"Look, mate, you leave every thing to me. Grab the paperwork and take me over to the fish factory."

Jim was waiting for them and it wasn't long until they had the dollars packed in the fish box and on to the pallet. There was only eight hundred thousand dollars this time so it fitted easily into one box. Danny left Bobo to wait on the London lorry. Danny went round to the office before he left and threw five grand sterling on the desk in front of Jim. This time Jim took the money with a smile.

"I think the wife and I will take a wee cruise, Danny, thank you."

Bobo phoned Mark and told him to hire a car and meet him at the fish market the next morning.

Danny went to Banbridge again to meet Bronagh. She had the kids with her this time. When the taxi pulled up Danny went over and took her and the kids back to the car. Danny sensed right away something was badly wrong. Danny got the kids into the car and Bronagh didn't get in right away. She spoke quietly and quickly.

"Danny, they are going to shoot you. Da came up last night and told me to tell you to stay away. He said Cathal Goodall has given the order that you are to be shot. Danny what are we going to do.?"

Tears were streaming down her face. Danny hugged her and told her to calm down.

"Look get into the car love and fix yourself. Don't let the kids see you crying, it's going to be all right."

"We got a new car, we got a new car." The kids were singing in the back.

Bronagh was so frantic she didn't even notice the car change. Danny drove to Cavan. They got to the country house and the kids ran wild through it. They loved it, they were on their holidays.

Bronagh had calmed down with Danny's assurances and began to look around. She started to tidy up and clean and then started to make dinner. Danny had brought in some shopping and Bronagh got to work. After dinner the kids went out to play in the garden.

A big light above the front door lit up the garden completely, the kids were wrapped up well and they played in the cold night air. Bronagh stood in the doorway with the baby in her arms, they were both well insulated. Danny had been running around with the girls playing every game they could think of until he was completely knackered.

After another half hour they all went inside and the girls and the baby boy were put to bed. When Bronagh came down stairs Danny poured them each a drink. "Bronagh I knew when I made my decision that it would come to this. The army rules are clear, misappropriation of army funds it's called. Maximum sentence, death, and when it's this amount of money they go for the max. I can't go back to live in Belfast in fact if I stay in Ireland it's only a matter of time before they find me."

"What are we going to do Danny what are we going to do?" Bronagh cried. "Bronagh I have a hundred and sixty thousand sterling here, by the end of the week I'm going to have almost seven hundred thousand and there is another two million dollars to fall back on, we can go where ever we like." Bronagh started to feel a bit better, now she realised there was a way out.

"Bobo is in London so while he is away I'm going to go to Spain and look for a place for us. I'll go out on a package deal and go and look for somewhere away from the tourist areas. We can rent first and after I've changed the rest of the dollars and laundered them we can buy a place. We can live like kings Bronagh we can live like kings."

Bronagh and the kids went back to Belfast two days later and Danny made arrangements for his Spanish trip. It was set for the following week and Danny started organising bank accounts and bogus businesses to launder the proceeds of the three million.

It took Bobo four days to change the eight hundred k of paperwork. Chomper and his mates worked hard and Bobo gave them ten grand each. Tony had agreed only to drive them around and didn't want any reward. Mark accepted the fifteen k that he was offered.

They still had the car that Mark had hired for the op, so the plan was to drive to Wales and get the Holyhead ferry to Dublin. Mark would drop Bobo off and take the car back. Bobo phoned Danny and told him he would be getting into Dublin around six thirty pm the next day and he told him he would meet him at the Silver Herring. Even though Bobo had met Sean there before he knew that Sean didn't normally frequent the place.

Danny was waiting in the car park when Bobo and Mark pulled in. Bobo got out of the car and opened the boot, he lifted two big sports bags full of sterling and threw them into Danny's car, neither of the two drivers got out and both cars were out of there in seconds.

Mark for the ferry and Danny for Cavan.

"Well how did it go over there Bobo?" Danny asked.

"No problem Danny Dee, no problem. Wait 'til I tell you something big lad, we can bust that other two mill in a couple of weeks time, and it will only take us ten days to do it. Those greedy bastards in those changers over there in London just can't get enough of dollars."

"Bobo, Cathal has hit me with a death sentence."

"What?"

"Yep mate. That's it, after my whole life in the movement they're gonna stiff me."

"No way Danny no way, look there's enough dissidents that have left the movement to start our own organisation, we'll take them on Danny we'll hit them first, the bastards."

"No Bobo, no, I've had enough, I'm too tired of it all. I'm going to disappear. Me and Bronagh have decided we're going to take off to Spain, we have enough money to grow old in comfort. I'll be sorting you out too because it won't be long before they turn on you, they'll knee cap you for sure and if Jamsey gets his way they might even stiff you."

"Bastards won't stiff me. I'll whack the whole lot of them in one night. I'll take them all out."

Danny had no doubt if Bobo went to town he could do a lot of damage but they would get him in the end, and Bobo knew that too.

"Look Bo kid, there's enough money here for a good life for us all. The kids would love to have uncle Bobo around them as well, so I was thinking, I'll go over to Spain and find a nice quiet spot, I'll rent a big place for me and Bronagh and I'll find a nice wee pad for you nearby. Look mate this could work out nicely. Think about it, a nice we flat, in a quiet wee Spanish village, wine for fifty pence a bottle, loads of wee sexy senoritas or in your case Bo, senoras."

The mood in the car started to lighten and Bobo had started to think along Danny's lines. Danny reacted to the news the same as Bobo when he had first got it, he wanted to take on the world, but after he had time to think he knew which was the best path to take.

All the way back Bobo kept talking about the new plan.

"Can you really get wine for fifty pence a bottle, Danny?"

"Yes Bobo."

"Here Danny, you know you can buy a rifle in Spain without a license, we could go out hunting."

"Yeah we could Bobo"

"Here Danny I could go round to your house and we could barbecue the rabbits and stuff that we shoot, and loads of wine, fifty pence a bottle."

"We could do that all right Bobo."

"We'll have to learn Spanish Danny."

"I suppose so Bobo."

"Danny how much dole money do they pay in Spain?"

"Bobo will you shut up for one minute you're doing my head in."

"Sorry Danny... Here, can I get a motorbike?"

Danny didn't answer.

"Aye, I'll get a motorbike." He said it more to himself than to Danny. Danny just smiled inside to himself.

Jamesy was delighted to get the news about Danny and went to work right away. He gathered his cronies together and put tabs on Bobo and Bronagh. Gary stayed with the movement, he new that Bronagh wouldn't come to any harm as long as he was there. He had appealed to Sean numerous times to lift Danny's sentence but Sean said he could do nothing, he thought he could sway Mick Rogers but Cathal was adamant. Sean had warned Jamesy that the row between him and Bobo was personal and that Bobo was to be left alone for now. Jamesy agreed with Sean but he had his own plans for Bobo.

Bronagh stayed at home most days and watched the cars that cruised past the door every now and then. She would go down to see her mum and dad two or three times a week. Gary had stopped telling her to get Danny to turn himself in after the death sentence was passed he knew there was nothing could be done. He also knew Bronagh was still in touch with Danny and just kept telling her to be careful.

    Danny booked a package holiday to Alicante and spent the week looking around. He had found a small town about forty miles inland from Alicante. The minute he drove into the town he knew it was the place. He found a Spanish estate agent who had a few properties to rent with the option to buy. Things fell into place nicely. He had a choice of six properties and he took a four bedroom villa with its own pool. It was just outside town, it sat on a half acre site with patios and gardens and it came with another four acres of rough farmland around. It was Danny's dream come true. He had also taken a small one bed room apartment for Bobo in the town centre. He paid the agent three months rent in advance for both places. He went back to Ireland and had brought back photos for Bronagh and Bobo to look at.

    Bobo came out of his house and spotted the two Stickies at the end of the street sitting in their car. He went down to the Falls and got a Black Taxi to the city centre the Stickies followed him. He got out of the taxi at Castle Street and walked the short distance to Castle Court Shopping Mall. The two Stickies were still on his tail as he got to the doors of the centre. He could see the passenger getting out of the car and going towards Bobo. As Bobo went in through the doors he made a dash through the crowded centre bobbing and weaving through the shoppers. When the tail got to the doors he could just see Bobo disappearing through the back doors. Bobo jumped into one of the minicabs sitting out side and told the driver to take him to the bus station. Bobo looked around and could see through the back window his tail standing with his hands on his head. He knew by the time he got round to the car the taxi would be long gone. Bobo got the bus to Newry and waited on Danny to come and pick him up.

Bronagh called a Taxi and took the kids down to her mum's. Eileen was always delighted to see them.

"Where's Da?" Bronagh said.

"He's round in the club," Eileen said.

"Mum will you keep the kids for me tonight? I am going to see Danny."

Eileen had long gone past telling her daughter it was too dangerous to stay in touch with Danny. She knew Bronagh would stand by him so she had decided to make things as easy as possible for her.

"Jamesy's two goons are sitting down the street there," Eileen said. "I know. They followed me down from the house. It's always the same," said Bronagh.

The two girls were watching television and the baby was asleep in the pram.

"Are you ready to go now?" Eileen asked.

"Aye"

"Right tell the kids cheerio and come out to the hall."

Bronagh kissed the girls and told them she would see them tomorrow. The girls didn't even look up they were too engrossed in the television.

Eileen and Bronagh stood in the hallway together. Eileen put on her bright red coat and hat to match. She set her hand bag on the hall stand. She walked out the front door and looked to the left for a good few seconds to make sure the boys in the car got a good look at her face, she then turned to the right and stopped suddenly and went back into the house. Bronagh was waiting in the hallway. Eileen quickly pulled her hat and coat off. Bronagh just as quickly put them on and grabbed her mum's handbag. She walked out the door with her face turned to the right. The boys bought it. Bronagh made her way down the Grosvenor Road to the taxi depot and got a taxi to Banbridge.

Eileen stayed in for the rest of the day and enjoyed her grandchildren.

Danny first went and got Bronagh and then picked Bobo up at Newry Bus Station.

They all travelled to Cavan together. That night Bronagh cooked three big juicy steaks with piles of steaming hot fried onions and mushrooms along with fat golden crispy chips. They sat down at the table and after they had eaten they began to talk about their new life. Bobo was still as excited as ever and had already bought a Spanish phrase book which he spent a lot of the night inflicting on the love birds.

"Right Bobo, we're off to bed."

"Danny we could buy two horses over in Spain, there's enough room to keep them at your house."

"Yeah Bobo maybe we will, good night."

Bobo didn't answer and Danny looked at him, as he sipped his glass of wine Danny could see he was miles away, in Spain sitting on his horse in the Spanish sun.

Danny and Bronagh lay in bed they both were as excited as Bobo, but Danny could sense a bit of concern in Bronagh's voice when she spoke.

"There's something wrong Bronagh, what is it?"

"Danny when I disappear to Spain that's it. That's it with me and mum and dad. I know I will never be able to see them again the movement would eventually find you through me. The kids will never see their grand dad and granny again. Danny I love you but it's going to be so hard leaving them."

"Bronagh it's all or nothing."

He listened as Bronagh cried herself to sleep.

Danny left Bronagh and Bobo off at Newry Bus Station, they got the bus to Belfast and then they got separate Taxis from the Belfast Station. Bronagh went back to Eileen and Bobo got left off a few streets away from his house and went in through the back alleyway.

Chapter 12

Danny booked a last minute flight to Alicante. He flew out the next day and hired a car to go to the villa. He stopped at a large shopping centre and started to buy stuff for the villa and some food and wine. He had told Bronagh he would stay for two weeks to get everything ready for her and the kids. The two weeks would also give her time to adjust and prepare for the big move. She wasn't going to tell Eileen until the last minute that she was going and she knew it was going to break her heart.

Danny was in the big living room, he had been working all day around the villa painting, fixing doors and getting the gardens in better order. He had just settled down to a well earned glass of cold beer when the phone rang.

"Danny, Danny, Goodall's dead, Cathal Goodall is dead."

Danny was stunned he knew Cathal was ill but he always thought the old IRA leader would live for ever.

"What happened was he shot?"

"No, no. Da said it was a heart attack it happened early this morning. Danny, Danny," she started to speak a little slower and hushed. "Danny, Da says Sean McStravick is taking over, he's in charge now. Danny, Da says Sean might do a deal, a deal to let you come back, he's going to talk to Da after the funeral."

Danny's head was spinning. He couldn't think straight he could tell by the excitement in Bronagh's voice that she thought that all their problems were over, but he wasn't so sure.

The funeral took place in Dublin two days later with all the trimmings of a military event and Sean gave the oration. Bobo didn't attend. After the funeral Sean came over to Gary.

"I'll come up to Belfast to see you tomorrow, Gary. We'll talk."

"Sean I beg of you with all my heart and soul I beg of you, lift the hit on Danny, Sean think of all that he has done for the movement over the years and Bronagh! Think about my daughter, and think about how much me and my family has done, please Sean, please."

Sean put his hand on Gary's shoulder and said "We'll talk tomorrow."

Sean was voted in as Chief of Staff right away, it was a foregone conclusion.

Danny knew there was a chance of making a deal with Sean and it wasn't long before things started to happen. Sean travelled to Belfast and went straight round to Gary's house. "Come in, Sean," Eileen said, she led him into the living room where Gary was waiting. "Do you want a cup of tea Sean?"

"That would be lovely thanks."

Sean got down to business right away. "Gary, Danny stole three million, three million dollars from the movement and we suspect he has killed two of the members. I am going to get it hard to put up a case for a reprieve. Mick Rogers is okay but there is a few in Dublin who are still thinking along Cathal's lines. It will be hard to swing them."

"Listen Sean, you know those two members that we're talking about were two informers. We could never prove it but we all knew they were selling out to the cops. It was only a matter of time before we whacked them ourselves. They were two cunts, Sean, two cunts. Danny did the movement a favour. It makes you think why Jamesy kept them around for so long. Sean,

Danny Devine was one of the best men we ever had, if not *the* best. You can't kill him you can't."

Gary was in tears, his whole body was shaking as he fell back into the arm chair he was sitting on. Eileen heard the commotion and ran into the sitting room and took Gary's head in her arms. She looked at Sean and could see that he was very upset two.

"Sean, you have to do something you have to, Sean, please."

Sean got up and handed Eileen a piece of paper, "Get this number to Danny, tell him to phone me at two thirty tomorrow afternoon."

Sean left Eileen and Gary with a little bit of hope. Eileen ran down to the Taxi depot and got a taxi up to Bronagh.

"Sean?"

"How are you Danny"

"Sean this would not have happened if Bronagh had been looked after while I was inside, for Christ sake forty or fifty quid a week would have done, that wouldn't have been too much to ask, forty or fifty quid, or even an acknowledgement if there was no money available."

"Listen Danny what's done is done, I can't turn the clock back, mistakes were made, and I still don't know the full story but we have to look ahead now. Where do we go from here?"

"That's up to you, Sean, what have you got for me?"

"Where's the money Danny?"

"I have it, well most of it."

"Danny you will never be able to walk around the Falls Road again, Big Luke and Mar--"

"Fuck them two touts, fuck them, they don't come in to this. I done you a favour."

"Okay, okay Danny, the money, if you're willing to give the money back we can come to an arrangement. You will not be able to come back to live in Belfast and as long as you stay away from the Falls Road I can give you safe passage. Bronagh can come and go as she pleases, she won't be followed or harassed. Maybe in ten years or so if I'm still around I may be able to fix it for you to come home for good. That's the best I can offer Danny, but you have to give the money back first thing."

"Sean, I can't come home. I'm going to be ducking and diving. My whole life is up in the air. I need money I need a place to live, I need to be able to see my family. This is my deal, and you can take it or leave it. If you don't take it then I put this phone down now and I just go ahead with my original plan. I have changed one million of the paperwork to sterling and punts. There is two million dollars left, and they are in a safe place. I will give you back the two million and you give me what you are offering now Sean. Take this deal Sean and I will tell you were the two million is, if you don't myself and Bronagh will disappear for ever with the money."

"Danny if I go back to Dublin with this offer they will be even more determined to find you and kill you. They need every penny they can get down there. Things are bad, Anton and most of his gang in Birmingham have been arrested, we lost a fortune over there, and the Yanks are trying to extradite me to the USA to stand trial. GHQ needs that money but they won't be held to ransom. Look, Danny, give me another half million worth of dollars in sterling. I can cover for the other half mill, if I tell the rest of the staff all the money has been paid back, I can swing it for you."

"Okay, Sean, it's a deal, and I will take your word on it. I'll give you the two million dollars first and then I'll give you the sterling in three weeks time when things have settled but one thing, I want to be able to go home now. I want to be able to take my kids where I'm going in peace and dignity. I want to come home even just for a short while Sean, have we a deal?"

"Okay Danny we have a deal. I'm so sorry it turned out like this Danny."

"Me too, Sean. Me too."

When Sean hung up Danny jumped up in the air and let a yell out of him. It couldn't be better. When he paid off Sean he would still have enough to buy the villa and have a good bit left to start a business in Spain, a wee bar or something, he wouldn't be able to buy Bobo his apartment, but he knew anyway, if Bobo was allowed to go back to Belfast, then three months in Spain would be enough for him. He would go back and straight down to the social security demanding three months back pay. The only thing is, he would be turning up at the villa every so often looking for cheap digs.

Danny phoned Bronagh and told her about the deal. She just could not believe that things had turned out so well she was overjoyed. She phoned Eileen.

"Mum, you and Dad come up here, it's good news."

Eileen and Gary arrived up at Bronagh's house within twenty minutes. As they came in through the door Bronagh ran to meet them and hugged them both. She explained the deal as best she understood it, and what Gary could understand from her excited talk everything was sorted and he knew that Sean's word was his bond.

"Get the champers out Bronagh, celebration time, get the Champagne out."

Bronagh brought out a bottle of Asti Spumante and three glasses, Gary did his best to make it pop as he opened it, and they all laughed as they clinked glasses and drank.

Danny called Bobo.

"All right mate, good news we're off the hook. I'm coming home tomorrow. I've got the last seat on a flight to Belfast, the flights at ten so I'll be home around two o'clock."

"Can you trust them Danny? It sounds too good to be true."

"Bobo I spoke to Sean myself, he gave me his word. In all the years we have known him has he ever broken it.?"

"No you're right Danny, but here, we're still going to Spain, aren't we?"

"Bobo we are still going to Spain and better still, we won't have to watch our backs every day. Be up at our house tomorrow before two, we have a lot of plans to make."

Sean met Jamesy in the Workers.

"Danny has been pardoned. I spoke with the rest of the GHQ staff this morning, and it was agreed, he is paying back all the money and he gets to come back to Belfast to sort out his affairs and after three weeks he has to move out. He can return to Northern Ireland at any time unmolested but will not be allowed to live in Belfast again."

"You must be joking, McStravick. I'll kill the bastard myself. You're a shower of stupid fuckers down there in Dublin, I'll kill him myself."

Sean grabbed Jamesy by the lapels of his Armani jacket. "That's the terms of the GHQ directive, if you go against this directive it will be you who will be executed. I'll pull the trigger myself you little shit."

Sean pushed Jamesy against the bar.

Gary walked in just as the bust up was ending. He knew right away what was happening but kept his cool.

"Listen Larkin, Danny's coming home so get used to it. Sean, Danny wants to meet you tomorrow evening to arrange the handover of the money. One more thing, Sean. At the next general meeting I will be proposing that prick's dismissal." Pointing at Jamesy. "I have evidence of money going missing from the funds for years now, and I think it's time to move on it."

Jamesy pulled himself together and stood up.

"I'm going nowhere. There's nobody can run Belfast like me so fuck you."

Jamesy went into the back office and banged the door behind him. Gary turned to Sean and shook hands with him.

"Thanks, Sean, thanks very much."

"No problem Gary. Look, in a few years I should be able to swing it that Danny can come back for good. Hopefully we will get rid of that little shit in there before then." Gary laughed, and lifted a cloth and started to wipe the bar, he was smiling.

Bobo arrived at Bronagh's house at one thirty. The girls were at school and the baby was asleep. The house had been cleaned from top to bottom, there was a welcome home banner up on the sitting room wall, and a small buffet on the table with a bottle of wine.

Bobo rapped the front door and walked in.

"Way to go Bronagh way to go, this all looks lovely." Bobo reached for a cocktail sausage and go this hand slapped.

"Nothing is being touched here until my Danny walks through that door." Then she smiled at Bobo. "Isn't it great Bobo? He's coming home." She turned and ran up the stairs to get herself pretty for her husband.

"We're still going to Spain though." Bobo shouted at the ceiling as he reached again for a sausage he bit into the sausage and muttered to himself. "We're still going to Spain."

Jamesy made a call and left the office, he was still seething. He got into his BMW and went to a house in north Belfast. He opened the front door of the small terraced house and ran up the stairs. He lifted the floor boards and pulled out a short fishing rod bag. He opened it up and checked the magazine of the folding butt AK47. The banana mag' held thirty high velocity rounds and it was full. He put the weapon back into the bag, went outside, got into the BMW and drove back over to West Belfast. He pulled up at a garage facing the Falls Park and crossed the road to the park he walked up through the park and could see his contact in the distance.

The two men met in the middle of the park. Jamesy handed the AK47 over.

"This is his address do you know where it is?" The ex-Provo declined the piece of paper Jamesy offered him.

"I know the house, I've watched it before. We were going to hit him ourselves a few years ago. I even have a spot for the hit."

"Okay, do it right and there is thirty grand in it for you."

"This is going to be a pleasure. That Bastard shot my best mate ten years ago, but I'll take the cash anyway."

The ex Provo walked back the way he came towards the Turf Lodge housing estate.

Danny's plane landed at Belfast Airport at one o'clock. And he made his way to arrivals. It wasn't long until his two bags came out. One contained his clothes and the other, three soft toys, Spanish donkeys, two big ones for the girls and one small one for the baby. It was twenty minutes to one in the afternoon. He went to the long stay car park and drove out. He didn't mind paying the massive parking fee; he was on top of the world.

As he drove down the airport road towards Glenavey he put his favourite tape into the player. Cathie Ryan singing, "Home Sweet Home" it couldn't be a better choice. He headed for home.

Danny drove into the small development and pulled up at his house. Bronagh and Bobo stood at the window looking at him coming towards the pathway leading to the front door. Bronagh could hardly contain herself she wanted to run out the door, but that would spoil the moment. She was going to pop the Champagne as he walked in the door. Bobo stood with a party whoopee in his mouth ready to blow at the same time...

Something happened.

Bronagh couldn't understand what Danny was doing. As he was about to open the small gate to the garden path he started to shake. He looked for a second that was doing some sort of silly dance. Then a split second later the cracks of the high velocity rounds told her what was happening. The AK47 continued to spit death and then stopped.

Silence.

Danny spun round and was still shaking as he fell back onto the ground. His clothes were in tatters, the life blood first burst from his veins each time a bullet hit a vital artery but now the blood just ebbed onto the ground. A red pool was starting to form just to the left of his chest.

Bronagh screamed but could not move as she watched the horror unfold. She was caught between disbelief and terror. It wasn't happening, it couldn't be happening. Bobo knew exactly what was happening. He ran out the door and reached the gate as the last report from the gun faded.

Danny was dead. He stopped at the gate, and looked down at his lifelong friend. Bobo bent down and lifted his hand and squeezed it. He straightened Danny's legs that were twisted in an obscenely ridiculous knot, he went in to the house and lifted a cushion from the settee and came back out to put it under his head.

Bronagh had started to move now. She was trembling as she took one short step at a time towards the door. Bobo sat on the ground with Danny's hand against his cheek. Bronagh's knees buckled as she reached the gate and Bobo jumped up to steady her. She moved over to Danny and knelt beside him, her life was over.

Rage swept over Bobo.

"Sean."

He got up and lifted Danny's car keys off the ground. He got into the car and drove down to his house in Clonard. He went into the house and out into the back yard. He pulled the bin over and lifted the loose tile and took out the large plastic box.

It was half twenty minutes before the police arrived and took Bronagh into the house a police woman sat beside her. Bronagh just staring at the window. A police man lifted the list of phone numbers from the phone table and dialled the number beside "Da's Work."

The phone beside the bar rang. Gary answered it while still talking to Sean.

Hello.

"Hello, sir. I am a police officer and I'm at a house I believe is your daughter's. She is in shock and we can't get her to talk, you see there has been shooting here and--" Gary dropped the phone and headed for the door. He ran round to his house to get Eileen. Sean followed him out and got into his car, it was parked around the corner from the club. He got into the car and started the engine. Bobo stepped out of the door way, tears ran down his face as he flicked the switch on the remote control. Sean's car lifted two feet off the ground, as it landed it turned into a fire ball.

Gary heard the explosion but was too engrossed. He was shouting at Eileen to hurry up and get into the car. They got into the car and drove towards the Grosvenor Road he passed Sean's burning car, Sean's body lay across the front seats and Gary didn't see it as he drove past. He stopped at the club and ran in. There was no sign of Sean and he went to the office. The door was ajar. Gary stopped then walked to the door slowly as he had just heard a joyful cheer come from the office. He stood beside the open door. He could see Jamesy on his big leather swivel chair with his back to the door, phone to his ear. "You're sure he's dead? You're sure? Good job, big son. I'll meet you later with the money, you can keep the AK." Gary went to the bar and lifted a rubber glove lying by the sink, and put it on his right hand. He opened a small panel. Danny's Webley was in the recess behind the panel. He took the gun and walked to the office and pushed the door wide. Jamesy spun round on the chair with a smile on his face. The smile disappeared as Gary pointed the big Webley at him. He emptied the gun into Jamesy's chest, the six heavy, low velocity slugs thudded into him. Dead. Dead as Hector.

Gary threw the gun to the side and walked out of the club. It was all over. He was going to spend the rest of his life looking after his young widowed daughter.

Bobo stopped at the liquor store on his way home and bought a bottle of whiskey. He knew that Mick Rogers would figure everything out in a matter of days, but he would wait six months to a year before he would have Bobo executed. So, Bobo decided he was going to spend that six months or a year in a drunken stupor while waiting for the bullet.

THE END

Printed in Great Britain
by Amazon